The Black and Red Rolls Royce

C.S. SIDAWAY

The Black and Red Rolls Royce
by Colin Sidaway

First published in 2018
by Colin Sidaway

© Colin Sidaway 2018

The moral right of the author has been asserted according to the Copyright, Designs and Patents Act 1988.

All rights reserved. No part of this publication may be reproduced, stored in a retrieval system or transmitted, in any form or by any means, electronic, mechanical, photocopying, recording or otherwise, without the prior permission of the author. This book is sold subject to the condition that it shall not, by way of trade or otherwise, be lent, resold, hired out or otherwise circulated without the author's prior consent in any form of binding or cover other than that in which it is published and without a similar condition including this condition being imposed on the subsequent purchaser.

A catalogue card for this book is available from the British Library.

Paperback ISBN: 978-0-9955472-4-7

Ebook ISBN: 978-0-9955472-5-4

Publication support

TJ INK
tjink.co.uk

Printed and bound in Great Britain by
TJ International, Padstow, Cornwall

CHAPTER ONE

Most stories could begin with a message in a bottle, and in one instance there was even a genie released from a bottle, but in my particular circumstances it was not a letter but a catalogue of a car auction. It had been delivered by post in a hand-written envelope. I didn't recognise the handwriting and was intrigued when on the front of the catalogue was a hand-written message:
See Page 8.

How odd. I put it to one side while I looked at my other mail: nothing more than an electricity bill that needed to be paid as soon as possible. It was later, while drinking a mid-morning coffee, that I picked up the catalogue again and indeed turned to page eight. And there it was: a 1929 Phantom I Rolls-Royce. I had another look; it was not only like the car that I had previously owned but, upon closer examination, I realised that it *was* my car. It had the same registration plate. There was no doubt about it, it was the car that I had previously owned and which held so many memories. I put the catalogue down and returned to drinking my coffee.

I had 'lost' the car in quite disturbing circumstances. I was intrigued. Did I want to put a bid in for it? I picked up the catalogue again to see that the auction was scheduled for two weeks hence. There was a reserve price on the car of £2,500. I wondered who would want to buy such a monster. I would, for a start, but where would I keep it?

Maybe I should explain that I am a retired diplomat and at that time lived in a Grace and Favour house in Bloomsbury. It was a rather large and spacious apartment meant for a family, not a fifty-something retired bachelor. The apartment didn't run to a garage. Some years previously there had been stables in a mews at the rear that had been converted into accommodation that was tasteful and lovely. A young couple had moved in. They worked in the City. Well, David did; I think that Angela was in the film industry. She was certainly attractive enough to have been a film star but I never asked and I never went to the cinema so I would never know.

The garage problem apart, I didn't have a car. I didn't need a car. I lived in London and everything I needed was right here. I would visit my club just off the Strand once a week for dinner, to meet up with old colleagues and possibly have a night away after reading *The Times* in the afternoon. On Sundays I would go for a walk along the Embankment or Hyde Park, or even Hampstead Heath on sunny summer days.

My only activity was to write the occasional letter to *The Times* regarding some point or other, on subjects upon which I considered that I had some detailed knowledge and which enabled me to pass on an informed opinion.

I picked up the catalogue again. I started with the envelope. It was posted in London the previous day. I still didn't recognise the handwriting. It was neat and well rounded. In fact it was written almost too perfectly. I racked my brain, trying to remember who knew that not only did I once have a car, but that *particular* Rolls-Royce. I was unable to recall anybody. My parents had known but sadly they were no longer with us. I checked the details again.

Yes, it was *the* car. It was a 1929 Phantom; the last car that Henry Royce had been involved with. It had a monster of an engine, 7668 cc with six cylinders. It had been fitted with a Pullman Limousine de Ville by Barker. It had some history but not a full history. More recently it had been 'found' in a barn and recently restored to its former glory. I wondered who that was as there was no information regarding the restorer or the owner. The car was being auctioned in Harrogate at the Show Ground two weeks' hence. I threw the catalogue into the waste paper basket in the part of the living room that I used as an office. My 'office' was only a roll top bureau. It was all that I needed for what little office work that I had.

A few days later I emptied the waste paper bin and picked up the car auction catalogue again. I thought that, just out of interest, I could catch the train to Harrogate and stay overnight and return the following day. It would be a rare trip for me out of the capital. I telephoned the Wagons-Lits travel people who made all the necessary arrangements on my behalf. In the interim period my thoughts kept returning to how I'd 'lost' the car in the first place.

I had been High Commissioner to a Central American Colony. I was there in the middle of a revolution that had been sparked by the neighbouring republic throwing out their dictator and seeing the opportunity to get rid of the British Colonial system in the same way. It didn't succeed and never would.

My car had been garaged while I was away. During the conflict at that time there had been an extended period where I was unable to meet the garage payments, and the car had been secured in lieu of payment. I'd had no idea that this had taken place until the uprising was put down once and for all. I came back to the UK to find that I had lost the one personal possession that I was sad to lose. What was even more upsetting was that I'd no idea who had bought it and there was no way of finding out.

This phase passed and I was knighted and given another High Commission on a Pacific group of islands. It was not as volatile as Central America but a quiet backwater of civilisation in the extremity of the British Empire. The reason for the colony had long since passed but it was still a relic of the Great British Empire. I'd put the matter of the car out of my mind. In the tropical group of islands under my remit, a car would have been the last thing that I needed; there were no roads, only boats to travel around the various settlements. Just getting there took the best part of eight weeks by various steamers. Apart from the telegraph, there had been little or no connection with the outside world. There were only local issues to come to terms with, and my legal background helped me with my staff, to give the controversial issues a well-balanced judgement. I'd thought and hoped that I was the face of the best of British justice.

The days passed and my thoughts kept returning to the Rolls-Royce I would soon see again. I asked one of my colleagues at the club if he knew anything about cars. I sought him out while at the bar.

'Hello, Sykes, I'm glad that I've met you. I have an idea that you have a Roller.'

'Jones, nice to see you again. No, no longer a Roller but a Daimler. I used to have a Red Label Bentley in the 30's that was a real bird puller and I took full advantage. Sometimes I wish that I still had it.'

'Can I buy you a drink? I am thinking about buying a Roller and would value your opinion.'

'That's very kind of you. Pink gin would be much appreciated.'

I ordered his pink gin and I took a schooner of sherry and we retired to two easy leather chairs that were very well worn.

'So, Jones, what's your interest in a Roller?'

'I had one just after the war and was separated from it due to circumstances beyond my control. It is now put up in auction in Yorkshire; the week after next.' I explained the story and gave Sykes the leaflet to look at.

While he was turning the pages of the catalogue I had the opportunity to assess Sykes and deduce the value of his opinion.

'Is this the one?' he asked as he arrived at page eight.

'Yes, that's the one.'

'It's hardly a bird puller. You aren't married are you?'

'No, I live in a Grace and Favour house over in Bloomsbury.'

'Well I'm blowed. What did you do to get that?'

'Serve my country. I was destined for a career in Law having taken a Law Degree in Cambridge.'

'How far did you get with that? I've never come across you at the bar.'

His question took me back to my time studying. I didn't mind giving him the abridged version of my career.

'No, I never quite made chambers. I was all set for going into the Temple with Talbot-Smythe but the war intervened.'

'My God! Did you ever meet Talbot-Smythe?'

'Yes, I went up to London for a sort of interview. My father was a GP in rural Norfolk and saw me in a white-collar profession but I wasn't interested in Medicine or Accountancy. I saw the law as being interesting and thought of following that but the war intervened, as I said, and I didn't quite get to the bar. Did you know Talbot-Smythe?'

'Know him? I married his daughter!'

'I had no idea.'

'It was that Red Label Bentley. I was over at Oxford and having a great time until I met Olivia, Talbot-Smythe's daughter.'

'Dare I ask?'

Sykes took a sip of his pink gin as he gathered his thoughts. 'I was reading Law and it was at a Law Society function that I met Olivia. She looked drop dead gorgeous and I succumbed to her smile and offered to take her out for a drive into the country at the weekend. Old Talbot-Smythe had no idea of the promiscuity of his daughter who had me in her sights and made sure that she caught me. At the time I had no regrets and it meant a route into chambers that I had not foreseen.'

I let him gather his thoughts before he continued with his story – he seemed to want to share it with me.

Sykes continued his narrative. 'Olivia was destined for the bar but had no intention of ever trying to fulfil her father's ambition for her to follow him into his practice. She saw me as a substitute, and how right she was. I was no sooner in her knickers than she had my ring on her finger and I was catapulted into chambers. Don't get me wrong, I wasn't complaining, far from it. I had my career planned out for me and I had a nice house in Caterham and a family to go with it.'

'So, it wasn't a bad result for you?'

'Hmm. I was dating four other women at the time and could have been engaged to any one of them. It was Olivia that netted me. This domestic arrangement didn't last long as the war came along and I enlisted, as you probably did.'

'Yes, before I could start with Talbot-Smythe I had enlisted for the Navy. No other reason but that I liked and missed the sea, having lived on the coast all my life.'

'I decided on the Army. I wasn't keen on being blown out of the sky or being in a floating tank that could sink to the bottom of the briny with me on it. With that thought in mind I joined the infantry and walked everywhere for the best part of five years. Every time I came home I had another child and left Olivia with another one in the oven.'

'How many children do you have?' I asked.

'Four. Two boys and two girls. They have kept me poor ever since.'

'I find it difficult to believe that you don't love your children.'

'Oh, I do love them, but having a house of teenagers is not high on my list of desirable activities. That's why I escape by coming here at least once a week. This is my respite from the lunatic asylum.'

'How was your time in the Army?'

'Tiring, in a word. I ended up in Italy. The Germans gave not one inch. Whatever we wanted we had to fight for and take. I walked the whole length of Italy. There were compensations: the Italian ladies were glad to see the back of the Germans and gave us the benefit of their gratitude. I was lucky not to get a dose of the clap. I think VD had more of a result than the whole of the German Army. Get a dose and you were on a charge.'

'Yes, we had that as well, but in my case that was unlikely to happen.'

'Why? What happened to you? Being a matelot you could have had a woman in every port.'

I smiled at his assumption. 'The only ship I ever saw was hardship. After basic I was sent to Chatham where I was given a Commission and a desk.'

'Lucky you. Walking thousands of miles with a forty-pound rucksack on your back and a rifle on your shoulder was not a Sunday afternoon stroll in the park.'

He finished his drink and stood up.

'Thanks for the drink. Let me know how you get on with your Roller. It's not a bird puller. You need to get a better image if you want to attract members of the opposite sex.'

'See you again, and I'll let you know how I get on. I'm not sure yet whether I'm even going to go to the auction.'

'Nothing ventured, nothing gained. Now I have to brace myself for another evening of domestic bliss. How I envy you.'

I stood up and shook his hand as Sykes turned and left me with the catalogue and some serious thoughts. I made my way to the dining room for my usual dinner of steak and kidney pudding with suet pastry. It was my gastronomic treat to myself.

After dinner I was drinking port with a plate of cheese when I decided that I would definitely go and pick up the details from Wagons-Lits the following day.

CHAPTER TWO

A few days after my evening with Sykes at the club, I went to the British Library Reading Room, hoping to pick up something, anything about the car, but there was nothing. On the day of the auction I took my first class seat on the 11 o'clock Flying Scotsman to York.

The train pulled out on the dot and soon was up to speed. The mile posts and telegraph poles seemed to fly by. I had a mid-morning coffee served at my seat and it gave me the opportunity to reflect on all the gaps in the information that I had given to Sykes. I had no idea that he followed his sexual desires. I never seemed to have had that sort of opportunity.

I had grown up on the north Norfolk coast where there were large skies and a silver sea with fresh breezes. My father was not well off. I don't think that GPs with country practices ever were, but as the only child I was expected to go to Grammar School and I managed to pass the entry exam. I had a life of homework, cricket, and rugby. I always wanted to kick the ball and not run with it under my arm, to be jumped on by all and sundry. I never made the school team in any sport until after passing my School Certificates when I was fifteen, and I stayed on to study in the sixth form.

There were a couple of things that happened at my grammar school that were significant. I became a prefect and then Deputy Head Boy. It meant nothing other than a convenient title but it did mean that I had to play for the school rugby team. I chose to work on being a scrum half – close to the action but not completely in it. I also played cricket for the school. I thought that they must be desperate as I plied my off spin as a bowler and batted at number 10. I didn't have many games and when I did I only had one stroke – forward defensive. I never made any runs but very rarely got out and left the run-making to others.

The other thing that became very influential later was that I joined the school cadet corps. For the first couple of years it was mainly marching around the playground come hail, rain or shine, but upon getting to the sixth form I had made Sergeant and then Second Lieutenant before a full Lieutenant in my last year as Deputy Head Boy. I also had to cram Latin and French so that I could have the desired languages to obtain entry to Oxford or Cambridge. No other university was even considered by my father, who stood over me as I crammed information into my head that could be released by answering the university entrance exams, which of course I passed. I chose Cambridge for no other reason than that I could travel home to Norfolk with just one change of trains. I settled into life in halls, reading and writing essays that seemed to be endless.

The lectures were boring and tedious and the tutorials were challenging and interesting. I struggled through the first year. It became obvious that, to get a good grade, I would need to put the hours in at the library and not the pubs or Students' Union where the beer was really cheap. I must have been really boring. I had no social life other than listening to discussions by others as they discovered the Classics and new mathematical solutions to unsolvable problems. I just listened and never spoke, as I had nothing to add to these conversations.

For an unexplainable reason I joined the Debating Society. What I didn't know when I joined was that once a year I would be called on to present an argument that would be discussed, dissected and voted on. I didn't have much choice in the matter as I was given the topic upon entering the chamber, so everything was off the cuff. The topic given to me was 'Socialism doesn't really work'. Ha! I had no interest in politics. I never had an original thought in my head. All I ever did was pass on a considered opinion that was somebody else's. I was glad that I didn't have to speak first and there was a real, live Socialist who gave the first arguments where everything would be the same for everybody possibly rounding everything down rather than rounding everything up. I argued that wasn't Marx's idea. What he considered was each to his own needs – which is not the same thing. It goes without saying that I lost the debate. It taught me not to enter into any discussion on anything without being thoroughly briefed beforehand. A good grounding for Law.

Reading Law is a tedious, head-in-books activity. I would spend hours in my room, in the library, sitting on the banks of the Cam, making notes that I could hardly read. The essays and dissertations came and went. My English improved considerably as I read my miserable efforts for my tutor, who was quite gracious as he marked me down with a C- or a D+. It was only towards the end of my second year that I got close with a B+, and then in my final year A's started to drop on my essays. My tutor went to great lengths to ease my progress towards the final year dissertation and final exams.

And then the end was in sight. My final exams were looming large, which were then followed by the vivas leading up to graduation. I had done my best and given everything my best effort.

They were frantic weeks and days before the Finals. My stress levels were at breaking point. I couldn't sleep at night and had difficulty staying awake during the day as I went through all my essays. wondering how I could turn all this hard work into a First. What would I do if I didn't? Could I live with failure, as I saw it?

To add to my misery, it was a really hot early summer. Long sunny days where other students were off on the punts having picnics on the Backs with lovely girls in gossamer dresses, laughing and having fun. I was in the library or my room in Magdalene getting as much into my head as possible, where the words seemed to enter and then get lost. The exams were in airless rooms and I became soaked in perspiration. This was not a good omen and I struggled on, more in hope than conviction.

The final event would be the May Ball that signalled the end of my time at Cambridge. My father had paid for everything without question, although had been living on next to nothing for three years. I more or less went cap in hand after my final exam to ask for £25 so that I could at least hire a black tie dinner suit and pay for the ticket to the May Ball. I had quite a surprise when an open cheque arrived in my post. What joy!

After the stress of the months leading up to the Finals and then going through the exams, there was nothing left for me to do other than relax and let my hair down. I spent a few quid in the Students' Union bar with my fellow hall students, and we were all looking forward to the high jinks that were promised at the May Ball. The rumours of pranks were flying high after the previous year, when three students from Magdalene had been sent down for skinny dipping in the Master's outdoor swimming pool in the early hours. They were obviously drunk. With written apologies, they were reinstated just in time for graduation. We had a high sense of anticipation as we dressed in our hired evening suits and drank half a bottle of whisky between four of us, to give us the Dutch courage needed for the ball. None of us were taking a young lady, we were all hopeful of finding a beauty who was also on the look out.

The ball itself had a large dance band in residence and the dancing was already underway by the time we made an appearance. There were couples standing around with drinks in their hands but there were twice as many men as ladies. The chances of meeting a willing or even unwilling partner were diminishing by the minute.

We each took a glass of champagne and my three companions made a circuit of the hall while I just stayed where I was, trying to take everything in. I wasn't the best dancer in the world and all four of us had practised with each other back in halls, hoping that nobody noticed and thought that we were a bunch of queers. Which, I might add, I definitely am not.

I saw a dark-haired girl by herself and plucked up courage to ask her for a dance. I put my drink down and turned and looked over, only to see that somebody had beaten me to it. She was smiling as she took the other man's hand as he led her onto the dance floor. Damn! The same thing happened again with a slim girl in an evening dress with long blonde hair falling naturally over her shoulders. This time I didn't look away, and started making my way towards her when this other man appeared from nowhere to whisk her off right in front of me. I turned away and went back to the bar and took another glass of champagne. This was not my night. I resigned myself to drinking champagne and looking on. I caught sight of the friends I had come with and they seemed to have found partners and were plying them with drinks. Lucky sods.

I was left alone with my own thoughts, not paying a great deal of attention to anything in particular. The compère announced a 'ladies invitation' waltz. I had no idea what that was until before me stood a lovely dark lady in a bright red, highly decorated evening dress. Her black eyes looked through me as if she could read into my very soul. She smiled a radiant smile, showing her perfectly white teeth hiding behind her two bright red lips. She looked lovely as she quietly said, 'Would you please dance with me?'

Would I? Damn right I would, whether I could waltz or not. I tried to smile back but I guess that my lips never parted other than to mumble something along the lines of 'It would be my pleasure, Miss.'

She took my hand and led me to the edge of the dance floor where I held up my left hand to take her hand in mine. She placed her arm over my shoulder and round the back of my neck, as she pressed herself to me. I put my arm around her narrow waist and she rested her cheek on mine.

'I'm not too good at the waltz,' I said, getting my apology in before I gave her a good kicking.

'There won't be much room for dancing. Just hold me close and move gently with the music.'

That was all that I could do. I was overwhelmed with the closeness of her body with mine, and the perfume in her hair filled my senses. I didn't hear any music or indeed realise that the music had ended. She was more than I had ever anticipated, expected or even hoped for.

She stopped dancing and released her arm from around my neck. I still held her hand in mine and her smile never seemed to slip from her face.

'Could you get me a drink, please?' she asked.

'I'm sorry, I should have asked. Thank you for the dance and what would you like to drink?'

'Orange juice or any fruit drink.'

I took her by the arm and led her over to the bar, where I asked for two glasses of orange juice. Once served, I tried to find somewhere to sit or stand.

'Can we have some fresh air?' she asked.

Wow, this was going all one way, was my only thought.

'Yeah, sure. There's a patio through the glass doors,' I replied, indicating the way out of the dance hall.

We made our way through the people standing around and talking, until the cool night air hit us. It was more refreshing out here and we found a low wall to sit on and sip our drinks. I was hopeless at small talk and didn't have a chat-up line in my repertoire of off-the-cuff remarks.

'What's your name? You can call me Nasri.'

'Nasri, that's nice. I'm Jeremy Jones. My nickname is JJ, after my initials.'

'Do I call you Jeremy or JJ?'

'The choice is yours. I will answer to both.'

She smiled again. 'You will always be Jeremy to me.'

This simple remark made me blush and I was pleased that it was dark; I hoped that she hadn't noticed.

'What are you reading and where?' Nasri asked. She was better at the small talk than I would ever be.

'Was is the word. I'm in Magdalene reading Law. I've just finished my Finals and will be going down as soon as I'm told that I'm not needed to hang around waiting for the vivas.'

'So, you won't be here next year?'

'No, I've just been studying Law and hope to become a barrister; hope being the operative word. What about you?'

'I'm over at Girton reading English. I've just finished my second year and have one more year to go. I'm sorry that you won't be around.'

'So am I but if I'm up in town, that's London, I'll only be a train ride away.'

'Jeremy, I need to be back in halls. Would you mind getting me a taxi or, if you can't get one, would you walk back with me? I don't like being out alone at night.'

'Who did you come with?'

'Just the girls from my dorm, but they have found interesting young men and I've found you.'

Again she made me blush. I felt foolish and embarrassed.

'Who did you come with? Were you by yourself or do you have a girlfriend?' she asked.

'I came with three of my friends from Magdalene. I've no idea what happened to them but I would be delighted to escort you back to your halls at Girton. I've never been there, in fact I think that in the three years I've been in Cambridge I've only seen the library, the lecture theatre and Magdalene Halls.'

'Are you a book worm or just a workaholic?'

'Neither. I think that I've been given a wonderful opportunity and don't want to squander it on the type of trivia that will always be just around the corner, should I ever want it.'

We collected her coat from the cloakroom and decided to walk back. It wasn't far and I had the opportunity to spend more time with the lovely Nasri. She took my arm as we sauntered along, neither of us seemingly wanting the occasion to be over quickly.

She was really inquisitive and seemed to have a host of questions that I tried to answer, like where did I come from? What did my father do? When was I graduating and when was I going down? I did my best to answer as clearly as possible until my curiosity overcame me at the Porter's Lodge, where the porter gave me suspicious looks.

'Nasri, can I see you again? I'm only here until the end of next week and then back for Graduation.'

She smiled. It was a smile of acceptance.

'Meet me by the Round Church opposite St John's on Sunday at about three, and we can hire a punt on the Backs and maybe have afternoon tea together. How does that sound?'

'Perfect. I will hardly be able to wait until then.'

She put out her hand to shake mine. I wanted more, but obviously this was not the time or the place so I took her hand in mine as we said goodnight.

I walked back to Magdalene in the cool night air. If there had been any drunken high jinks they had not come my way. I felt as sober as a judge, yet strangely elated. I had met a lovely young woman who really wanted to see me again. It would be my very first date! I didn't sleep that night. I was full of apprehension and self doubt. What if she didn't like me in the cold light of day, especially out of my dinner suit and wearing my old corduroy trousers, holey sweater and Harris Tweed jacket? I had never been boating on the Backs. I was soon going to get my baptism; hopefully a dry one.

The following day there was the usual inquest: who did what with whom and what was the resulting outcome. It appears that my fellow students had tried to have their wicked way with girls they had picked up, only to be either given the cold shoulder or left high and dry when boyfriends turned up. They were intrigued by my meeting with Nasri but I had nothing to report other than we had had an orange juice and I walked her home. The subject quickly moved on to more interesting topics, including relating the silly antics of the drunken fringe who had decided to walk over the roofs back to their respective halls. It was a well known event that I never believed but had truly happened evidently.

When Sunday came around I walked around my room. I was the

proverbial cat on hot bricks. The hours dragged and so did the minutes, until two o'clock came and suddenly time speeded up and was flying by. I rushed to get ready and put my jacket on and pull a brush through my hair. I hoped that I looked appealing to the lovely Nasri.

It was only a short walk for me to the Round Church and I arrived almost to the minute. There was no sign of Nasri. At least I wasn't late and didn't keep her waiting.

The time passed and with each minute my heart sank. I would be stood up on my very first date. Depression and self-doubt started to creep into my inner self. I had never been in that place before. It was something that I would have to get used to.

It was close to half past three when Nasri came. She was dressed in traditional Indian dress with trousers and a colourful top, and a silk scarf. She was accompanied by an older man. She came straight over to me, took me by the hand and kissed my cheek.

'Thank goodness you are still here. I'm sorry to have kept you waiting. This is my father's idea: me having a chaperone for the afternoon. Nothing I could do about it but at least I'm here. I hope that you don't mind.'

'Mind? No, I don't mind. I'm just pleased that you are here now,' I confessed.

'Having Dev with us, I thought that the boat trip would have to wait. Can we just go for a walk over Jesus Green and hope to find a tea shop? Tea will be on me as I have kept you waiting.'

We linked arms and walked into the City and through Jesus College to Jesus Green, being followed by Nasri's minder, the ever-attentive Dev.

'You never told me that you were Indian.'

'Sorry, I thought that was pretty obvious. You don't mind being seen out walking with an Indian girl?'

'No, why should I? I could ask you if you don't mind being seen with a down-at-heel Law student.'

'You would get the same answer. I think that you are a handsome young man and any girl would like to take my place on your arm.'

'I'm afraid that's a figment of your imagination. This is my first ever date, would you believe?'

'Now I find that hard to believe. If that is the case, I feel highly privileged. Look, there's a small café over there with tables outside. Dev can pay and my father will reimburse him later.'

She led me to the café where she ordered afternoon tea for two. The tea came with scones, strawberry jam and cream. I wanted to pay for at least my share but she would hear nothing of it.

I asked about India and her father. She said that she was Hindu and was the only daughter, in fact the only child, and she wanted to be a teacher when she returned to India. I guessed her father was well off to be able to afford to send his daughter to university, and not just to any old university but to Cambridge. I asked her what her father did. Her reply was a surprise. 'All that he seems to do is worry about me and his cars. He arrived last week and is going to the Rolls-Royce factory next week where he wants to see his cars being serviced to his satisfaction.'

'Cars! How many has he got?'

'I don't know. I haven't counted but he seems to collect them. There aren't any roads to any great extent where we live but he likes the prestige that seems to go with them.'

'My Dad has a car,' I said. 'It's a 1935 Morris 10. I learnt to drive in it. He will be coming to collect me next weekend so I have a week in which to pack everything up. I will send most of it by rail. I think that it would be too heavy for the car.'

She laughed at my little joke before becoming serious. 'I will have to return to India with my father. It will take something like four weeks taking the steamer from Southampton. He refuses to fly. I will only be home for a month and I will have to make the return journey back here. I think that the faithful Dev will be with me. Father thinks that I need a chaperone.'

'And do you?'

'And do I what?'

'Need a chaperone.'

She smiled. 'Only where you are concerned. I've not met anybody as nice as you, but I need to tell you now that I have been betrothed to an older man since I was twelve.'

'I see,' I said slowly. 'So when will you marry this man?'

She sensed that I was going cold on our friendship and this was just our first meeting. She reached over and touched my forearm.

'Jeremy, I guessed that would upset you but I had to take that chance. I would never be able to lie to you and wouldn't want to. I have no idea when the marriage will take place. I think that my father is putting together a suitable dowry. I've no idea how much it is likely to be but I think that at least one of his cars will be part of the settlement.'

'Are you happy with that?' I asked. The whole concept of arranged marriage and then paying somebody to take your daughter off your hands was a complete mystery to me.

'What does happiness have to do with anything? It is a tradition in my country that has been part of life and living for centuries. My liking or disliking it has little or no consequence. It seems strange to me that people here in the West marry just because they love each other. I could ask you the question: what has love got to do with marriage? Most married people that I've met are not happy, or would you disagree with that?'

She was now questioning my Western concepts. I found that strange as up until that moment I had not even given it any thought. I didn't reply immediately as I tried to recall all the happily married couples that I had met. None of them seemed that happy with wives giving husbands grief over minutiae. I had no idea about my parents. They were just there. I had no idea whether they were happy or not.

'Cat got your tongue?' Nasri asked.

'No, I'm just thinking of what you have just told me. I think that you are probably right but I don't think that I could marry anybody that I didn't love and respect.'

'Ah, now it's more than just love. You have added respect. Are there other things you would like to add?'

I thought for a moment. 'Honesty, faithfulness and being trustworthy.'

Nasri burst out laughing. 'Your list is never-ending. Do you expect to ever find a wife with all those attributes?'

'I was hoping that I had just found such a person, who then tells me that she is not only spoken for but has every intention of marrying somebody she has little knowledge of and, and, and... I don't know what else I can say.'

'Jeremy, that's the nicest compliment I have ever had. I will always try to be those things to you but I have no say in who I will marry, as it is all arranged and has been for many years.'

This brought not only our conversation to an end but also the afternoon tea.

'Jeremy, I have to go. You need to stay here. Dev will report to my father who disapproves of me seeing anybody. How can I contact you?'

'Leave a note with the porter at the Magdalene Lodge and I will pick it up. Anytime this coming week would be fine. As much as I don't like the thought of you marrying somebody else, I really want to see you again.'

'And I you. I will try for later in the week. I will drop a note with a day and time to your porter. Next time, can we meet inside the church and not outside, just in case I'm early or you are late.'

I nodded my acceptance of the arrangement.

Nasri stood up, as did the ever faithful Dev, who settled the bill and gave me a dark and surly look. Nasri never looked back but just walked ahead of her minder as she returned to wherever. A few minutes later I left the café and took a long walk along the Backs. What was I even thinking about with this Indian woman who I guess was more than a doctor's daughter? If her father had several Rolls-Royce cars he must be some sort of prince or maharajah, which would make Nasri a princess in her own right. I vowed that I wouldn't see her again.

What a stupid vow that turned out to be. The following Wednesday I picked up a note from the porter which simply said: *Thursday. 2.30.* I couldn't wait to see her again. I wondered if her minder would be with her. I would find out.

The following day found me surrounded by my attempts at packing all my things. Saturday was moving day for me. I was twenty minutes early at the Round Church, so much for my vow of not seeing Nasri again. I found a pew at the rear of the church near the entrance. I sat, trying to wait patiently but without much success, kneading my hands with anxiety. Today Nasri was a few minutes early. I didn't see her come in. I became aware of her presence when she stood behind me and put her hand on my shoulder, and I had a whiff of her very distinctive perfume.

'Jeremy, I'm so glad that you are here.'

I spun round to see Nasri, not in her traditional dress but with her hair put up under a hat, and with no make-up. She wore a jacket over a loose sweater and slacks. This was not the princess of my dreams.

'Nasri! You look more like a boy than a girl.'

She smiled. 'That was the idea, and my way of getting out without the devoted Dev escorting me. I just want to be alone with you for a couple of hours.'

So that was the reason she was dressed as she was. I stood up and confronted her. Even without her make-up her smile was captivating and her dark eyes were like jet, reflecting what light there was in the church. I had fallen for this girl big time. I'd heard it said that your first love stays with you forever. At that moment I didn't know that, but travelling up to York on the train thirty years later I reflected on it, only to conclude that I had not loved anybody before or since as I did at that moment.

We walked hand in hand along the Backs on a lovely warm early summer afternoon. We arrived at a small park and sat down on the grass to watch the children on the swings, their mothers circling them, protecting their offspring from the dangers of falling.

I was at peace with the world. I lay back with my hands under my head and watched the little white clouds go scudding across the sky.

'What are you thinking?' Nasri asked.

'I'm thinking about you and your life here and how far it is away from your palace in India.'

'Oh, so you've guessed. I suppose it was me telling you about my father and his Rolls-Royce cars.'

'Something like that. Why didn't you tell me rather than let me work it out for myself?'

'If I had told you, would you be here now with me, as just two people enjoying the simple pleasure of being in each other's company?'

'No, I guess not,' I replied. 'I'm just an ordinary man with some sort of ambition that is not my father's but mine. Falling in love with a real live princess is something out of fairy stories and not real life. I would never have been able to walk out with you holding your hand.'

She leaned over to me and put her lips on mine, giving me a soft warm kiss. What was she doing? And what was I doing letting her and responding to her? I rolled over and half lay on her as I returned her kiss with an ardent passion that seemed to start with my toes turning up, until my whole body became rigid with pent-up passion.

After just the one prolonged kiss I lay on my side. looking at the lovely Nasri.

'Take your hat off. I want to see your hair,' I said.

She gave me a smile and sat up to remove her hat and release her hair. It was thick and black, and not only cascaded over her shoulders but half way down her back. She was truly a lovely princess, my princess.

'Is that better for you?' she asked.

'Nasri, I have fallen in love with you,' I confessed.

She leaned across to kiss me again. 'Jeremy, I loved you the moment you took me in your arms at the ball.'

This was all too much. We lay together, just kissing and stroking each other's face and hair, as the minutes swiftly passed and turned into over an hour.

'Jeremy, I need to return before somebody starts a witch hunt looking for me.'

I stood up and helped Nasri to her feet. There was little or no conversation as we walked back to Girton. I had my arm around her shoulders and she put her arm around my waist so that we could walk as close to each other as physically possible.

'Jeremy, when are you going down?'

'Sunday. My father is not on call out and will drive over from Norfolk to collect me and my belongings. I will be saying goodbye to Cambridge. When are you leaving?'

She sighed. 'When my father is good and ready is the simple answer. I don't know but probably next week sometime, possibly Monday. What's the number of your room at Magdalene?'

'17. Why?'

'I will try to get one of Daddy's Rolls' for the afternoon, possibly Saturday, so don't go out.'

'I won't be going out. I've no money left for a start, and I can't see how I can get everything into the boxes.'

'I don't have that problem. I have servants to do that for me.'

At that moment I realised that we were not only nationalities apart but lifestyle, custom and religion. It was a chasm too far for me to breach. She would have to come to me. I then realised that it would be too much for her as well. We were doomed as would-be lovers. I would make the most of what little time we might have together.

'I do want to see you again. I'll wait in the hope that you will call.'

'Just in case, can you give me your home address so I will be able to write to you?'

'If I don't see you, I will drop the note in to you at Girton.'

She smiled her response. What I didn't know or realise then was that she would never be able to pick up my note or any mail sent to her under her familiar name of Nasri.

At her door, she squeezed my hand and then put her hair up into her hat, turned, and almost ran away from me.

I slowly walked back to my room, changed and went for dinner. Many undergraduates had already left and I had no company for the evening. Having little or no money meant an evening of packing and reading.

Saturday, after the apology that was lunch, I was lying back on my couch wishing that I had the money to buy some cigarettes, and thinking that home cooking would be most welcome, when there was a knock at the door. I went to see who was calling. I hoped to see Nasri but instead it was Dev, dressed in a dark suit and tie.

'Memsahib has requested your company,' he said.

'I'll just get my jacket,' I replied, and took my coat from the back of the door. I followed Dev out to the street where I saw the Rolls-Royce for the first time. It was huge, mainly red with a black bonnet and mudguards. It was parked directly outside the main entrance doors, totally blocking the entrance, but I didn't think that anybody would even consider asking for it to be moved.

Dev opened the rear door for me to enter. Nasri was sitting in the far corner greeting me with a smile. 'Thanks for coming,' was her greeting.

Today she wasn't the scruffy street urchin, but my princess. She wore a scarlet dress with gold and silver threaded patterns, inlaid with blue and white sapphires. Pantaloons and a gossamer thin scarf draped around her head completed the look. Her hair had also been fashioned with braids that hung around her shoulders. Her lips were painted bright red and her mascara only highlighted the blackness of her eyes. I think that my jaw dropped.

Dev sat in the front alongside the driver and we set off, on a journey I knew not where. But did I care? I did not!

Nasri had closed the sliding window dividing the rear passengers from the driver so that we had privacy. She took my hand in hers. Words were not forthcoming. They were not needed. We were two people in love and only desired to be in each other's company. Well, that was my take. I could have been completely wrong but this only confirmed that I had lost my heart to this beautiful young woman.

The car purred along, making even the bumpiest of roads as smooth a ride as I could ever have imagined.

'Where are we going?' I asked as I realised that we had left the city behind and were heading out into the countryside.

'For a picnic, an Indian picnic. I hope that you will like it.'

What was there not to like? I was silenced, overwhelmed by the occasion and circumstance.

The car entered a large estate through wrought iron ornate gates, and drew up alongside a pool that was surrounded by weeping willows. I had no idea where we were. Alongside the pool was pitched a gazebo with table and chairs for two, with a silver service tea set laid out already prepared for us.

Dev opened the door for me and then I helped Nasri out. She gave me a smile and uttered no word of thanks to Dev. He was in her service and knew his place.

We walked the short distance to where tea had been prepared. We were not expected to serve ourselves; two waiters dressed in white uniforms appeared as if from nowhere to pour tea and serve us sandwiches and small sweet cakes.

'Have you eaten today?' Nasri asked. I guessed that she realised that I had reached the end of the road, not only for studying but also money.

'No, not really. I'm looking forward to going home where I can have a decent home-cooked meal.'

'Just eat your fill. This really is all for you so enjoy my little gift to you.'

I probably ate more than I should have, but the sight of good food that was tasty and spicy was too much of a temptation. It released my tongue and a whole load of questions that I wanted answered.

'Nasri's not your real name, is it?'

'No, it's what my family call me. My real name is far too long for you to remember, but I will give you all my contact details when I write to you in Norfolk.'

'You truly look beautiful today. I'm overwhelmed by you.'

'Jeremy, I'm still the girl that you took to the park and kissed, but sadly there won't be any kissing today. I'm on my best behaviour and would ask you to respect that.'

'It seems as if I have fallen in love with two beautiful people. Different yet the same person.'

'I love you too, and don't really want to leave here, but I'll be back in September for my final year and we can go on seeing each other.'

'I look forward to that.'

'So will I.'

Tea came to an end.

'We have time to have a short walk along the edge of the lake, if you like,' Nasri offered.

I stood up and took her hand as she got up from the table, and I offered her my arm as we strolled along the grass verge. I was unaware of it but the tea things were cleared away, and the car and the ever-present Dev waited for us to return.

We chatted about Cambridge and our studies. I was worried about my grades. Nasri was not in the least concerned about hers. She would be coming back regardless, and if necessary would be awarded an honorary degree if she failed, though that was unlikely to happen. That's what you got when you had wealth and privilege. I had neither; I had to rely on hard work and ability. I smiled to myself, thinking back to my debacle at the Debating Society when I had tried to make a case for such privilege and the Socialists won hands down. By comparison, I too was a Socialist but didn't begrudge the well-off what they had. It seemed to me that they were prisoners within their wealth.

Back at the car, Dev opened the rear door for Nasri to enter, and when we were sitting comfortably the driver slowly pulled away, heading back to Cambridge. But instead of going to Girton or Magdalene he drove to a large five-star hotel on the outskirts of the town and pulled up outside the front door.

Nasri gave me a nervous smile. 'You now have to pay for your afternoon tea with me. You have to meet with my father.'

Damn, I thought, that's all I need. I had little choice but to follow

Nasri up the front steps of the hotel where her father was waiting for me. God, I was being introduced to Indian royalty! The ground could have opened up at that moment and swallowed me.

I stepped forward to meet the maharajah. He was dressed in a dark suit, white shirt, and what looked like a club tie of some description.

He held out his hand and I offered him a firm grip with mine as I bowed my head in recognition of his status.

'I'm pleased to meet you, Sir.' I had yet another panic. How do you address a maharajah? I had no idea and hoped that 'Sir' would be sufficient. Little did I know, but he was used to such a lack of formality and etiquette while he was England, and accepted my introduction.

'And I am pleased to meet the young man that my daughter has befriended.'

I didn't respond to this, but waited for the inquisition to start. I realised that Nasri had left and we were alone.

'I take it that you like my daughter.'

'Yes, Sir. She does you credit and you should be proud of her and her achievements.'

'She tells me that you have been reading Law.'

'Yes, Sir.'

'Do you expect good grades?'

'I think my life depends on the grades I manage to get.'

It raised a smile on the older man's lips.

'Tell me, do you like cricket?'

'Yes, Sir, very much. I was in my school cricket team but I have been too busy studying here in Cambridge to advance my career in that direction.'

'Did you bat or were you a bowler?'

'Off break spin bowler, Sir. I only ever had one stroke with the bat and that was forward defensive.'

Again he smiled. 'Cricket is my passion. If you ever manage to get to India, we will have a game together; the Maharajah's Eleven against a scratch Cambridge Eleven. What do you say?'

I was beginning to like this man and he was putting me at my ease. 'Sounds like a challenge that I wouldn't be able to resist.'

'Come and sit with me and tell me about yourself. Did you like my car that Nasri took you out for a drive in?'

'Yes, Sir, very much. I passed my test in my father's 1935 Morris 10 which is not quite in the same class as the Rolls.'

'I love cars almost as much as I'm passionate about cricket. I have six Rolls-Royce cars. I've had them some time and I needed them checked over at the factory. One day, we will make cars in India but that day is a long way away, I'm sad to say. The British Raj wants to keep the status quo and I'm happy and content with that, but I don't think that you British will keep a hold on India when it wakes up from its slumbers. Have you heard of Ghandi?'

'Isn't he that South African fellow who is throwing his weight around?'

'More like asserting his rights. He's a clever fellow. A lawyer, don't you know, but being anything but white in South Africa is a heavy burden to carry. Not so much in India where our population is based on a caste system that not even the British could break. Tell me, are you interested in politics?'

'No, not really. I tried to debate against the Socialists in the Debating Society and was heavily defeated so I think that I am better suited serving the law and offering considered opinion rather than actually thinking and implementing original concepts and ideas.'

The maharajah listened to my little speech and lit a cigarette. The smoke drifted upwards as he sat back, evidently weighing me up.

'You realise that Nasri is betrothed to another.'

'Yes, she has already told me.'

'Does that give you cause for concern?'

Ah, at last he was getting round to the main item on his agenda.

'I don't really grasp the concept of arranged marriage but accept that it is a well known and well-practised tradition in your community. If you are really questioning me as to whether I respect and honour your daughter, I do and always will. I think that I know my place and, as devoted to her as I am, I have no intention of breaching her or your trust in me. Now, I think that I have to return to my rooms. My father is taking me home tomorrow and I am unlikely ever to see Nasri again. Can I say that it's been a privilege and honour to meet you, Sir?'

'And me you. I can see that Nasri has good taste in choosing her companions. The car is outside and will take you back to Magdalene.'

I had been dismissed. I turned and left the older man to his cigarette. The car was indeed waiting for me but there was no Dev. I had to open the car door myself and sat on the grey cloth bench seat. Nasri's perfume still hung in the air as the car made swift progress into the centre of Cambridge. I was pleased to step out into the fresh air and turned into the college as the Rolls-Royce sped off.

Back in my room I sat on the edge of my single bed and buried my face in my hands. I had really fallen for a real-life princess only to be told that we could never be together or even see each other. I was a lost soul in a wilderness that I had never seen or appreciated before.

My depression was all-encompassing. My father fussed around putting my bags in the boot and on the back seat of his Morris. He had no idea what had depressed me but just thought that it was probably nothing more than a post-exam anxiety attack. It was that as well but somehow that didn't seem to matter as much anymore. What an emotional state I was in.

Mother was pleased to see me. She noticed how thin I had become and considered that I needed to be better fed, but I had little appetite for food. What I needed was the love of a good woman, the love of Nasri, and that would never be forthcoming.

Things moved along in what seemed to be a snail's pace. I received the exam results, which resulted in a First that pleased Dad. Mum was proud, and I just accepted the accolade. Now that I had the result I was persuaded, cajoled would have been a better description, to attend the interview in the Inner Temple.

Cometh the day, cometh the man. I took the early train from Norwich to Fenchurch Street Station. I was dressed in a new suit that Mother had insisted I had for the interview, and I found my way from Fenchurch Street to The Strand where I entered The Inns of Temple.

There were more than several chambers of barristers and I followed the instructions for how to locate the chambers of Talbot-Smythe. It was like stepping back into the London of Dickens; everything was brown and dark. I was shown into an office that had book shelves filled with the law as written.

The interview went well, I thought. Talbot-Smythe was everything that I had expected. He was tall and distinguished, in a dark suit that I was sure he had worn every day for the past twenty years. It wasn't much of an interview; he just looked at my exam results. I would be taken on as a junior to see how things turned out. I was aware that it would all be down to me. Barristers were either 'in the business' through family connections or you had to be talented and brilliant in your own right. I was beginning to think that I had neither of these attributes.

The law courts were closed for summer and my duties would commence in Michaelmas. So I had the summer to find some accommodation and get ready for court life. I would also need a gown and wig.

That was not to be. World events overtook me and the country. It was early in that September, 1939, that war was declared. I enlisted immediately.

CHAPTER THREE

Sitting on the Flying Scotsman heading to York and then onwards to Harrogate, I recalled that Father was delighted that I had enlisted. Mother was concerned and worried that her only son was off to sea. I had enlisted in the Navy and was accepted, I was glad to say.

I was extensively interviewed upon being accepted. My cadet corps rank and training at school held me in good stead, and that I had an education in the classics and languages also went in my favour. I was offered a commission but needed to take an intensive course at Devonport. It was mainly to bring me up to speed with things nautical but they insisted I had an intensive course in speaking and writing German. I had no idea why; that was just the Navy way evidently.

So my two months in Devonport saw me leave with gold rings on my sleeve. I must admit I rather liked the look of me in the naval officers' uniform, and it brought tears to my mother's eyes when I had leave before taking up a posting.

Father's pride excelled and he was disappointed on two fronts that he couldn't enlist. The reasons were that he was deemed too old and, being a doctor, he was in a reserved occupation and would be needed on the home front.

My posting came as a surprise. I was requested to report to Chatham: they had given me an office job. The only ship that I would ever see would be through an office window.

The British Navy was in no shape to take on the might of the German Navy. We were out-shipped and out-gunned. The threat was great indeed, and the war effort was not a case of sailing around, but of getting what we had up to speed and working to bring on new ships as quickly as possible. We just didn't have the capacity and my job was to cajole Whitehall into providing men and equipment as quickly as possible.

We seemed to be alright initially. We could keep most of the German fleet in the Baltic as they only had one real port on the North Sea. That containment was overcome when France was entered through Belgium and, within a matter of weeks, the Germans had ports on the Atlantic coast that included submarine pens. They were intent on cutting off our supply lines.

Requisitions came onto my desk like confetti. I consolidated the items and was then put on the train to London, and then on to the Admiralty. Post was too slow and could be intercepted or even destroyed in a bombing raid. Spies were said to be everywhere and not seen or noticed. Twice a week I would go to Trafalgar Square and into the Admiralty with my list.

I had a small staff in Chatham to help me sort out the logistics and I quickly had a promotion up to Commander and was transferred, directly working in the War Office. My understanding of French and German came into their own as I was constantly asked to translate messages that had been picked up and decrypted. The work was intense and seemingly never-ending. My legal background was also in demand, drawing up contracts for the supply of goods and materials, and, later, inspection of the factories and shipyards as well as the supply chain.

The work was round the clock. I managed only a few hours' sleep. Working nights surprisingly was the easiest; buried in the Whitehall bunkers while London above us burnt. We would emerge each day to see what damage the bombing had caused and to have a nap, sometimes in St James's Park on a bench if it was a nice day, or in my cot in the Admiralty building.

We were losing shipping faster than we could replace it. The other services were also suffering but I had more than I could cope with just with naval affairs.

I rubbed shoulders with the Chiefs of Staff as well as being called in to No 10 to listen to Churchill giving out his orders. I was also a frequent visitor to the committee rooms in the House of Commons, listening to argument and counter argument, pleased that I wasn't making choices and difficult decisions, but just carrying them out to the best of my ability.

The days merged into weeks, months, seasons and years. We were slowly winning the war, or so we were told. Being in the thick of things in Whitehall, none of us had any idea, but there was no choice or let up. The work had to be done and we were there to see that it was.

When the Americans came into the war, they too had demands.I seemed to be trying to do the impossible, namely get the American Navy to follow our lines of operation, but all they seemed to want to do was hit the enemy with everything they had at their disposal rather than use what resources they had to maximum effect.

The air raids on London became less frequent and there was a party atmosphere in the city each and every day and night. The West End, although in darkness due to the blackout, still had a vibrant nightlife. I saw little of such high jinks other than occasionally having a beer in the Army and Navy Club, meeting up with real sailors who were in transit from one yard to another or changing ships and having a few hours at home with loved ones. I managed a forty-eight hour furlough every three months or so, and upon one occasion collected a letter with an Indian post mark that intrigued my parents. It was on the personal stationery of the Maharajah Margit Singh. It was from Nasri. It was short and confirmed my worst fears.

> *Dear Jeremy,*
> *I am here in India and won't be returning to Cambridge. I have their reading list and I just have to submit a written essay of my choosing, then I will receive an honorary degree. I was so looking forward to seeing you again but this wretched war has taken its toll on everything and everybody. I hope that you are safe and I pray for your wellbeing, hoping that one day we will meet again.*
> *Your loving friend*
> *Nasri*

I screwed up the letter. At least she was safe in India. Surely Japan wouldn't expand their empire in that direction. I could only hope, but, knowing the Japanese, if they had taken on America they must have thought that they were invincible and nothing was beyond their colonial ambition.

Mother came and asked if everything was alright. I showed her the letter.

'Was this your girlfriend?'

'No, not really. I had only met her at the May Ball. I also met her father who spelt it out to me that she was beyond me and had been betrothed since she was twelve. Nasri was definitely off limits.'

'She seems to have taken a liking to you, to have written you such a nice letter.'

'Yeah, sure. She befriended a poor hard-up student who was in total awe of her. Little did she know that I would fall in love with her. There you have it. Unrequited love is about as bad as it ever gets and it has hit me hard. The Navy is my saving grace. I need to work as hard and as well as I possibly can so that we come out of this mess the world has got itself into.'

Mother put her arms around my shoulder and kissed me on the side of my head. 'She wasn't for you, but what I do know is that there is a girl out there somewhere who is. All you have to do is find each other.'

It was a consoling thought, but one that for some reason I didn't buy.

That mood of isolation stayed with me for almost as long as I worked for the Navy in the Government. There were parties where Wrens would be invited as officer fodder; pretty secretaries that provided more that secretarial services whether they or their partners were married or not. Make love tonight as you might never see tomorrow, so don't concern yourself with things that far ahead.

I seemed to work at least eighteen hours a day and it was only once or twice that I woke up with a woman I had only met the previous evening and would be unlikely ever to see again. It provided some sort of physical satisfaction but really all it did was get the anger out of my system for a short time; anger at not being with Nasri, who by now was married to some other man and at his will and calling.

I was still emotionally messed up and saw that the Navy and war effort were my only salvation.

VE day came and was celebrated like no other. I think that day the population took a big step forward. I just had a quiet drink in the Army and Navy Club with my fellow officers and colleagues. We still had a war to fight. The Japanese were still there and were not giving up. The Americans were fighting their way across the Pacific and we were joining in with the ANZAC troops and Indian Regiments to take back

Singapore, Malaya and Burma, as well as a host of Pacific Islands under our Colonial protection.

I was despatched to Bombay and then on to Calcutta, where we had a strategic HQ. It was there that I came under the direct command of Mountbatten.

He seemed a genuine sort of man who only wanted the best for everybody, and the Japanese back in Japan where he considered they belonged. The Japanese Navy was a formidable opponent and our deployment of the Atlantic Fleet was also despatched to take up the mantle in that area of conflict.

I was flown down to Darwin and then on to Canberra where I sat in on the meeting with the Australian Chiefs of Staff, sitting alongside Mountbatten as we listened to the arguments that they would put forward to the Australian Parliament for approval and money. It seemed to be a repeat of everything I had previously heard in London. I left with Mountbatten to fly back to Calcutta.

On the way back we were sharing a drink and he asked me: 'Jones, what do you think about this theatre of war?'

'I don't think, Sir. I leave that to politicians and yourself. I sometimes offer my considered opinion. Nothing more and nothing less.'

'You sound like a lawyer.'

'With respect, Sir, I have a First in Law from Cambridge. I think that's well developed in my psyche.'

'So it is. So what do you think?'

'We have to bottle the Japs up and restrict their lines of supply. That's the Navy's task but they will only ever be beaten on the land which is not our immediate problem. Keeping the ground troops supplied I think is an Air Force problem. We need at least another couple of carriers so that we can provide air protection and support to the supply chain.'

'I think that's about right. Why didn't you speak up at the meeting?'

'Not my function, Sir. I was only an observer, as we both were. You asked me what I think and that's what you have been given. How we achieve these things are decisions that you and the politicians have to come up with. I will always be on hand to implement whatever actions are needed.'

'Ah, you are there to assist the executive right or wrong.'

'Yes, Sir.'

Back in Calcutta I saw little of Mountbatten or his entourage, as the war in Burma proceeded at an alarmingly slow rate until the Americans, fed up with having their troops killed on every beach on every island, dropped just two bombs and suddenly the war was over. I was left helping with the tidying up, where all our fleet was scattered. It was another two years before I hit the shores of Blighty. My medal tally had grown and the gold rings on my sleeves had become broader. I was higher up the command chain and had yet to serve on a ship. Such was the way of the world.

I was close to being discharged when I used what contacts I had made over the years, especially in Whitehall, with a view to going into the Diplomatic Service. I had some good backers in the Atlee Administration and also from the Navy through Mountbatten.

I was summoned to his office one day in the Admiralty and duly presented myself.

'Ah, Jones, I see that you are still in harness.'

'Not for much longer, Sir, I'm hoping to go into the Diplomatic Service.'

'Yes, I was aware of that. Take a seat and listen carefully. This is straight off the desk from No 10. You get my drift?'

'Yes, Sir, not a word even to my dog, if I had one.'

He smiled. 'Exactly. This Labour Government, as you know, are nationalising everything in sight. They are also dismantling the Empire.'

'My God!' I exclaimed.

'Yes, it's all in the pipeline: Canada, South Africa, Australia and India. The smaller territories will make their own way. I've been asked to oversee India in the transition.'

'Do I congratulate or commiserate with you?'

'I think that I would take both. I want you on my team and hope that you would take this opportunity to advance your new career in the Diplomatic Service.'

'Thank you,' I replied. 'I would be delighted to help in whatever way I can. Would I still be in the Navy? I think what I am asking is whether I would need to sign on for a further term or take my chances on Civvy Street?'

'I'm hedging my bets. I have signed a new contract for three years.

It will take that to sort out India and I have the choice of buying myself out or staying. Could I suggest that to you?'

'I think that you have made a wise choice,' I told him. 'As and when I am offered an extension to my present arrangement, I will give it due consideration.'

Mountbatten smiled. 'I see the lawyer is still in you. I think that you will need that in spades dealing with the Indians.'

I stood up. I guessed the meeting was over.

'Can you give me some sort of time scale in which to sort things out of a domestic nature?'

'Things are moving quickly. Everybody is up for this and want the whole thing done and dusted in the life of this Parliament while Labour have a commanding majority. So three months at the most. I will be flying out next week. You might just get a call within the week so be prepared.'

'Thank you. I look forward to the challenge that this presents.'

I left his office and returned to my own, where I put in a request for a forty-eight hour weekend leave. I would go and stay with my parents for the weekend and take stock of my present situation. I also put in a request to see my immediate superior with a view to getting clarification regarding my role and term of office within the Senior Service.

I had the meeting before my weekend at home. My present arrangement had been open ended and this was an opportunity for me to add a completion date. After taking my contract and reading it again with the eyes of a lawyer, I put in a termination date of 31st December, 1948. That should be enough time to get the foundation of a new India sorted out, and the rest would be down to the locals and out of the British sphere of responsibility.

I went home for the weekend armed with the news. Father had been interested in my work in the War Office but I felt that he was disappointed in me as I had not seen active service. Sitting in a bunker through the blitz didn't seem to count somehow.

Mother was just pleased to see that I was fit and well, yet she was disappointed that I didn't have girl on my arm and her dreams of grandchildren were still a million miles away.

I enjoyed being in civvies and just walking up and down the coast, finding a pub and having a glass of beer. I had home-cooked food off the meagre rations that we could buy. I gave Mother my ration book so that they could get larger portions of everything. It made life just that little bit easier.

Dad tried to draw me on my present work and was surprised that I had signed on for another three years. I tried to explain that it would benefit my pension but I don't think that it was a defining argument. I think that he still wanted me to walk into court as a barrister. I was determined more than ever to go my own way and carve out my own career. Doing Law had been his idea. Going to Cambridge had been his desire. Getting a First Class degree was his pride. None of this mattered to me. Even going into the Senior Service was what he would have liked to have done and I was living and fulfilling his dream and aspirations. I was now going on thirty and at last was about to start to fulfil my own ambition.

It was later the following week that I received the call: report to the Admiralty Office for further orders.

CHAPTER FOUR

Changing trains at York reminded me of the train journeys I made while in India. The journey from York to Harrogate just rattled along a suburban line, making frequent stops. We were on a no corridor train and there were no first class compartments. Rather than sitting next to the good and the great I was sharing a compartment with a pipe-smoking rotund man who seemed to be typical of the unwashed and poorer community that travelled along the branch line to Harrogate and beyond.

I was quite smoke-infused when I alighted at Harrogate and made my way to the Majestic Hotel. That too reminded me of my days in India in the dying days of the Raj. It was Edwardian on a grand scale that was both classic and elegant. I felt at home in such surroundings.

I dropped my overnight bag in my vast room and ordered a taxi to take me to the preview of the auction. I was duly taken to the Pavilions on the Show Ground. I showed my programme to the attendant on the door who allowed me to pass, to where all the classic vehicles were being inspected by would-be experts. I doubted whether any of them knew everything about every vehicle on display.

I sauntered along the line of vehicles. There were one or two veteran models as well as a Red Label Bentley. I wondered whether I should put in a bid for and on behalf of Sykes. I gave it my attention: there was a back seat but it really was a sports car on the grand scale. I was sure that Sykes really didn't need the back seat but would be happier sitting behind the wheel with a cap put on back to front and wearing a pair of goggles. I was sure that he cut a glamorous figure, attracting ladies both young and old. Would I have the need of such a monster of a vehicle? I thought not and I couldn't even begin to imagine the grief he would get from his wife if he turned up with the Bentley in its British Racing Green. I moved along.

Then there it was; my Rolls-Royce. It looked the same as when I'd first seen it some thirty years before, when it had just come from the factory. It was immaculate and definitely not like the car that had been in my possession. I slowly walked around it. I was mainly interested in the back seat for – how can I delicately put it? – for personal reasons. The upholstery had been completely replaced to the exact condition as I remembered. It must have been a costly exercise. I looked again at the suggested price of just £2,500.

'Can I interest you in the details of this car?'

I had been approached by a rather young dashing salesman, or did he belong to the auction house? He was dressed in tweeds and I guessed he was more used to selling farm equipment and tractors rather than facilitating the two classic car auctions they held every year.

'I'm intrigued by the restoration,' I confessed.

'Ah, it was coach built in 1929 by Barker of London as a Pullman Limousine de Ville for an Indian Maharajah.'

'Maharajah Margit Singh.'

'Ah, you have heard of the gentleman.'

'I have met him on several occasions. But tell me more about the car and the restoration.'

Not thrown by my admission, he continued with his well-prepared narrative.

'The car came back to England sometime in the 1940's.'

'1948 in the November, but please continue.'

The auctioneer gave me a strange look, wondering how I knew so much about the car and its previous history.

'Well, it ended up in a garage that went bankrupt and the vehicle was put into storage. It was more or less left to rot until it was found, and no expense was spared on giving the vehicle a total rebuild of the engine and refurbishing the interior exactly as Barkers had built the car back in 1930.'

'1929,' I corrected him.

'1929. Since its restoration it was recently tested on a hundred mile trip. The car performed very well and had good oil pressure and cool running. We have written confirmation from the company that did the restoration that the chassis is also in good, sound condition. Can I say that at the expected price of £2,500, it would be a sound investment to a collector? Do you have a car yourself?'

'No, I don't. I live in Central London where having any sort of vehicle is a distinct disadvantage.'

'Oh, I thought that you might have been a collector. You seem to be very knowledgeable about this car.'

'This car, yes, but interested? I'm not so sure. I will need to make up my own mind. So who is the present owner?'

'I'm sorry but I'm not allowed to disclose that. We don't want you making a private offer outside of the auction, if you understand my meaning.'

'I understand your meaning precisely. You are looking to get a good commission and don't want anybody making a private deal to deprive you of your income. So what is the sort of percentage you would be looking for?'

The young man coughed. I don't think that he had been prepared for a direct question regarding his financial interest but somebody had to pay for the hall, the publicity, etcetera. I guessed that it would be me as well as the vendor. I reasserted my point. 'If I made an offer for the vehicle, what percentage of the purchase would I then be required to pay the auctioneer? I take it that you are the auctioneer so don't hide behind your financial requirements.'

'Seventeen and a half percent.'

'And the vendor?' I asked.

'A similar figure.'

So, Mr Smart Alec Auctioneer was making thirty-five percent on each car sale. Well, that was his business and he seemed to attract both car sellers and buyers so it must be a good business. I wondered what he actually made. I guessed I would never find out.

'Tell me about warranties,' I said.

Again, he coughed. 'None of the vehicles in the sale carry any sort of warranty.'

'Ah, buyer behold! I'm not surprised, but what chances are there of either a test drive or my own private inspection?'

'I think that you would need instruction before driving the car. It is very specialised and has a few idiosyncrasies that you wouldn't find on modern cars. Sadly, at such a late stage, we don't have time for any detailed inspection.'

'Buyer beware comes to mind again,' I replied. 'Would you like to show me some of the idiosyncrasies or would you like me to explain them to you?'

'I don't understand your meaning.'

'Thirty years ago I had both the pleasure and misfortune to drive this very vehicle, and unless I have a loss of memory I recall more or less every detail down to actually changing a wheel.'

The auctioneer was stuck for something to say but excused himself as he had spotted a less knowledgeable victim.

I walked around the car again. The doors were locked and I could only peer inside. It was in absolute mint condition. I would have something to mull over during dinner.

The surroundings of the Majestic and seeing the black and red Rolls-Royce again brought my memories flooding back: memories of my return visit to India to work with Mountbatten. Flooding was a good word for them, as I'd arrived in the rainy season. I had never experienced rain like it, it rained incessantly, but then suddenly one day it stopped, to return again the following year. India really was a strange place...

I settled into quarters set aside for me in Government House and I duly presented myself to Mountbatten in my white tropical naval uniform.

'Ah, Jones, good to see you again,' he greeted me. 'Rather sooner than either of us expected no doubt. This whole thing is moving along at a rapid rate. The time scale has been dwindled down to a few months rather than years.'

'Where do you want me to start?' I asked, avoiding any small talk.

'The British Government, well the Civil Service, have drafted out a constitution that Whitehall is pushing for. I need you to go through it and then take it to Ghandi; have you met him?'

'Yes, Sir, during my previous tour of duty.'

'Then you know what you are up against,' he said. 'When you have got that past him we will be sorting out everything else under the British control and passing on to an elected Government. Have you any idea how many people will get the vote? God knows how it will be organised and hopefully they will come up with their own solution, as just putting the elements of Government will be taxing enough.'

'Very good, Sir.'

He handed me the document that had Top Secret stamped all

over it. 'Gandhi is presently in New Delhi. It's not safe for me, you, or anybody here in Calcutta at this minute. I suppose that you have heard about the partition.'

'Not in detail,' I replied. 'Why are we trying to separate the Muslims and the Hindus?'

'Simple: they hate and mistrust each other. If we don't separate them into their own independent countries there will be all out civil war and millions would die for no purpose. The bottom line on the deal is that Gandhi has to agree to the partition to get independence. No agreement, no independence. You have to take that message to him. I think you have an affinity with Gandhi, he was called to the bar at the Inner Temple. Does that ring any bells with you?'

'Yes, Sir. If the war hadn't intervened that's where I would have gone.'

'At least you have some common ground,' he said. 'Now get your skates on. I can't guarantee your safety here in Calcutta. I'm moving out myself to follow you up to New Delhi as soon as I possibly can.'

I saluted, took the constitution and, with it under my arm, returned to my room. I instructed my boy to collect everything together as I made my way to the main railway station. There were protest marches going on but I was unable to work out who was protesting about what. The inspiration seemed heavily religious. Maybe partition really was the only way out. I caught the next train out to New Delhi. It was an overnight and a whole day following to make the capital. I had more than enough time to read the paperwork. It seemed fair, and set out a constitution that was based upon British Law and Institutions which, although never put down in words, was not all bad. This was going to be as close as anybody was likely to get. I wondered whether the same constitution would be the model for the Muslim partition. It was a discussion point with Gandhi.

Upon reaching New Delhi I took a tuk-tuk to the largest hotel in the place, had a shower and changed my clothes. After a meal, I felt almost human again.

Next morning, dressed in my naval whites and with the new constitution in the document case under my arm, I took a taxi to the Government building. There were scenes of total chaos, or apparent chaos. As with everything in India there never appeared to be any sort of organisation about anything but, strangely, things did get done and were achieved. I tried to make an appointment with Gandhi but nobody seemed to be able to help me. I decided to look for him myself and, without being stopped, walked through the corridors of power, looking in each and every room I came to. I eventually found him sitting in the garden in his loin cloth and a sheet draped around his shoulders, spinning some cotton. The man whose very presence had the sub-continent on a knife edge was sitting quietly. I guessed it was his way of working things out in his own mind.

'Sir, Mr Gandhi, Sir, I'm Commander Jones, British Royal Navy. I hope that I'm not disturbing you.'

The little man looked up from what he was doing.

'Jones, I've been expecting you. How did you find me? With difficulty, I guess. Come and sit with me and give me the bad news first.'

I sat alongside the great man, cross-legged on the floor.

'I'll cut to the chase. The British Government will give you independence if you agree to separation of Muslims and Hindus into two different states.'

He momentarily stopped spinning.

'Jones, in this life you never get what you want and most desire without compromise or making some sort of sacrifice. What do you have to show me?'

'A draft constitution.'

'What does it say?' he asked. 'Are you some sort of lawyer? I've met you before, during the war, I believe. So why are you here now? You are a long way from Chatham, or would it be Portsmouth?'

'Yes, Sir, we have met before. Then we were both on the same side, and now I think that we are both fighting our own separate wars. I only spent a short time at Chatham and spent most of the war in a bunker under Whitehall. If the war had not intervened, I would have followed in your footsteps by going into the Inner Temple.'

'They never told me that. So you are a lawyer first and a naval officer second.'

'Sir, the only boat that I have ever been on was the steamer coming here during the war. The Navy has a logistical arm as well as manning ships.'

'So,' he said, 'tell me about the constitution.'

'Would you like me to read it to you?' I asked.

'No, not really. What does it say in simple language?'

'It's more or less a copy of the British unwritten constitution. It's not on the lines of the American model that was drawn up by Adam Smith, another English emigrant. It states that all men have fundamental freedoms and rights, such as to vote for an elected assembly and freedom of speech.'

At that point Gandhi started laughing as if I had made a joke. I didn't get the joke or the humour.

'That's a good one, Jones. I've been arrested and jailed for my free speech but yes, it's good and needs to be in there. I think that we have enough of our own lawyers to pull it to pieces and put it back together again without the British Civil Services stretching their imagination. So, what's the time scale, do you know?'

'No, I'm not privy to what Cabinet decide but I believe Atlee is all set to nationalise everything in sight and give independence to India, Canada, Australia and South Africa, and a load of other smaller states that it sees as being a burden that the country could do without in very bad financial times.'

'Yes, I've heard that as well. The British papers get here weeks late if at all. We should be at the centre of the British Empire, not a backwater. Without wishing to offend you, I have been campaigning to get India out from under the heel of the British for twenty years and at last I am just a whisker away.'

'So I believe,' I replied. 'I tried to debate in the Cambridge Union on the merits of free enterprise and against Socialism and was trounced in my arguments. Now we have a Socialist Government these values will be tested, but as far as India is concerned I don't think that Socialism will break the caste system.'

Gandhi gave me a look that tried to work out my motives.

'Sir,' I said, 'I am just the messenger in this instance. I don't make decisions but can give my considered opinion and, having seen the bloodshed and religious riots only two days ago in Calcutta. I think that separation would be the lesser of the evils.'

'I think that you are right and it is my decision. I hear daily of the bad feeling between Muslim and Hindu communities. It will be upheaval for many millions of people as whole communities would be uprooted. Do you have any detail of the separation?'

'None at all, Sir. I only arrived from England three days ago and have only had a brief conversation with Mountbatten.'

He nodded thoughtfully. 'I think that he is a good man who has been given a poisoned chalice and he has passed it on to you. Come back tomorrow and I will give you my answer. Now, are you going to leave me with the constitution?'

'My instructions were not to let it out of my possession but I think that I can misplace it for a few hours. It really is bedtime reading. It put me to sleep on the train.'

I handed Gandhi my document case. I realised that in the frame of this old man lay a greatness that I was only ever likely to see once in a lifetime. He was a man of his word and I believed him.

I stood up and left him to continue spinning cotton.

Back at the hotel, I put a call to Mountbatten to give him an update, telling him that this time tomorrow I would have Gandhi's decision. In one way he was pleased but I could sense his frustration that the old man would not yet commit himself.

I had an evening of little or no sleep in an airless room that left me covered in perspiration. When it was hot in India it was *hot*, and this was the north of the country. I couldn't imagine what it would be like in the south.

Next day, in a clean uniform, I made my way to the Parliament building where I found Gandhi again sitting spinning his cotton thread. It would be an everlasting memory for me of the great man.

'Ah, Jones, come and sit with me,' he said.

He continued spinning his cotton as I sat alongside him.

'You were right, the constitution is tediously boring but it will give our lawyers something to chew over.'

I didn't ask or push for an answer to the unasked question.

'I have also made a decision regarding separation,' he continued.

I waited, wondering what the decision was. It was almost like a judge pronouncing his findings on a difficult divorce case.

'The price for independence of separation is accepted in principal,' he told me.

'You have reservations and would like some sort of clarification?'

'Yes, exactly right. You are a smart young man and I wish that I could negotiate with you and not those clowns in Whitehall, but I value your opinion, especially as I think that you are going in to bat for me.'

'Mr Gandhi, Sir,' I said earnestly, 'I have taken the King's Shilling. I only serve my King and country. I have no political opinion or any gains to make in that direction, but what I would want is a more definitive proposal on the separation, and safeguards regarding two constitutions and not one. I'd also try to get money and assistance in training, both military and civil, in the running of a new country. I don't think you would get any money out of Whitehall as they are broke, but they have a great deal of knowledge and I think that we both know that knowledge can be both powerful and rewarding.'

'Yes, I had concluded that as well. Great minds seem to think alike. I don't understand why you seem to be an Indophile.'

'At Cambridge I fell in love with the daughter of a maharajah who was beyond me in status and wealth. I have always looked on India in a favourable light. Having the opportunity to serve here and stop the Japanese empire expansion gave me a love of the country and the people,' I told him.

'Are you married to a fair English maid?'

'No, Sir. I am not. I don't think that anybody could replace my first and only love.'

'Well, it seems as if I have you batting for me. I will hear how Mountbatten takes the news as he will be here next week. I think that your job will have been completed then, and he will find you another task, of which there are many here in India. Thank you and goodbye, Jones. I wish you well.'

I had been dismissed. I stood up. My document case was lying next to Gandhi. 'May I take my draft?'

'What draft? I have seen nothing.'

'And it has never been out of my possession. Goodbye, Sir. I hope that you get the independence that you have devoted your life to achieve.'

I turned and left the Government building, and returned to the hotel to make my phone call. Mountbatten was delighted and said he would sort out the detail to put to Gandhi the following week when he would be installed in Government House. He would find me another project to fill out my time in India.

CHAPTER FIVE

I had a couple of days seeing more of the city and the various temples that seemed to be scattered around the countryside. It was during the following week that Mountbatten sent for me and I duly presented myself to him.

'Ah, Jones, you did a great job with Gandhi,' he told me. 'He was receptive to our overtures and his demands, although significant and comprehensive, we could accommodate. Since then I have drawn up a map for the separation. The new Muslim state will be called Pakistan and will itself be separated into east and west. Millions of people need to be moved and that's our biggest problem. India has something like thirty small states that need to be brought on board. So in the next few months each will have to be visited by would-be diplomats to bring them into line. I have included you on the list and have selected one for you. It's only half a day on the train from here so you can be brought back if we hit a negotiation problem.'

'What's needed in the states?' I asked.

'Oh, it's like our local elections, They all have their own language, which is their problem; the good news is that they all speak English. They are ruled by petty princes and maharajahs whose influence will be greatly reduced as national law will override the local petty laws that they dish out from time to time. They will also have to have regional representatives in the National Assembly as well as local people sorting out local problems. There will be a new wave of Socialism sweeping over the country and that needs to be contained. That's your job. I guess that there will be other things that need sorting out when you get there but I have every faith in you and will only want the occasional progress report. Now, I must press on.'

I was again dismissed. I picked up a folder to see where I was expected to go. It appeared that I was a Naval Officer land-locked with not a ship in sight. It was yet another step for me on my diplomatic journey.

I repacked my bag and took the train ride up into the foothills of the Himalayas. It was mainly a tea-growing region and, from looking out of the carriage window, seemed to be quite affluent; that is, affluent on an Indian scale. The little train chugged into a small station that just had the name written in Hindi with a small English translation, *Jurihadnapur*. Try saying that on a Saturday night.

I found a tuk-tuk and requested to be taken to the hotel. I guessed that they would only have one and I was right. It was not grand on a large scale but was grand in the English manner of trying to be opulent without being overly ostentatious. I checked in and found a large airy room that looked out over a valley, where the folds of deep green hills disappeared into the distance. This was likely to be my home for the next few months. I unpacked and made my domestic arrangements with the hotel manager, who almost grovelled as if I was some big white chief. He was also my only contact with the movers and shakers in the district. My first port of call would be to the local maharajah. The manager ran away and made the arrangement for me to meet the maharajah the following day at four, for tiffin. I really was in a backwater but I guessed that there were twenty-nine other regions just the same scattered over the sub-continent.

Seeing the main man in the afternoon gave me the opportunity of exploring the town. There was a daily market where everything seemed to be out on the street. Well, it really wasn't a street, just strips of land between houses and shops. Everybody I met had a smile for me and I was followed everywhere by brown urchins with sparkling eyes and big smiles showing their white teeth. They were mainly in rags and I had no idea why they were following me. I was told they wanted me to give them pennies and that would get rid of them. I was dubious about that as, if they thought I was a soft touch, I would never get rid of them.

After a light lunch I had an early afternoon lie down. It was the only way to get through the hottest part of the day and the sun was unrelenting in its ferocity.

At four o'clock I duly presented myself at the palace and was shown into a room that was cool and airy with walls decorated with blue and white tiles. It was very grand and obviously belonged to the main man.

After a short wait I was ushered into yet another room to be introduced to the maharajah. I had a double-take. It was Nasri's father! I wondered whether he recognised me. I guessed not.

'Commander Jones at your service, Sir.'

'What's a Naval Officer doing here in the middle of India?' was his opening remark.

'My superior officer is Mountbatten who is also a Naval Officer. We live in changing times, Your Highness. You will soon be free from the shackles of the British and will have your own Parliament to deal with.'

'Yes, I've heard about that,' he said, looking at me closely. 'Do I know you? You seem awfully familiar somehow but I can't think how that could possibly be.'

'You obviously don't remember and I'm not going to remind you. You have more important things to consider.'

'Such as?' he asked.

'What the British couldn't achieve in a couple of hundred years Gandhi will achieve in a matter of months. It is the end of the Raj.'

'Nonsense.'

'As you please,' I said, 'but I was with Gandhi only last week and he is currently negotiating separation of Muslims and Hindus into separate states. You need to identify your Muslim families and make arrangements for their exodus, and also make arrangements to take Hindu families from areas within the new states.'

'Hmm. It will never work.'

'That is not a question that you or I can answer, but when the Indian Army march in here and forcibly evacuate whole families I would not like to be in your shoes. If you want my opinion, and I am going to give it whether you heed it or not, you should co-operate with Central Government whether you believe in their policies or not.'

He shook his head sadly. 'I thought the British were bad, imposing their so-called values on us, but I can't believe that is the price we are paying for independence.'

'It's what you have been crowing about ever since your predecessors sold out to the British. Now you will have elected representatives of the majority of your people and they will have their demands for schools and hospitals met, and taxes to pay for them.'

'I hate politicians. Where do you stand in all of this or are you just the profit of doom?'

'I'd never seen myself in that light,' I told him. 'I thought that I was helping a friend through a difficult period of transition.'

'Since when have the English ever been philanthropic?'

'We play a fair game of cricket, and that gives certain values of honesty and fair play, or do you make up your own rules here on the sub-continent?'

'What do you know about cricket?' he asked.

I ignored that question, deciding I would return to it at some future date, maybe. I continued. 'We also gave you standards to live up to, like providing superb buildings and engineering. Do you still have your Rolls-Royce cars tucked away in a garage somewhere while children run around the streets with no shoes, whatever rags they could find to wear, and no school to go to? I think that you need to get with the game before the game overtakes you.'

'What do you know about my Rolls-Royce cars?'

'Nothing, other than you have no roads to drive them on. I will bid you good day and I daresay we will have many meetings in the future. But I think, next time, you will be calling on me at *my* convenience and not yours.'

I turned to go away and leave him. The boot really was on the other foot and I wouldn't kowtow down to him again.

Outside his palace, I felt happier and more content with my lot. I would knock democracy into this little bit of India and it would be my pleasure.

The days that followed were interesting as I located the regional meeting chamber that would be elevated to the regional government building. I also had the opportunity of meeting the leaders of the political parties; there were twelve of them. I listened with interest to their manifestos, that ranged across a breadth of local grievances that needed to be addressed. I explained to them that there would be national elections that would mean their representatives would be sent to New Delhi. I had a meeting with the heads of the Muslim community and gave them the news that they would be getting a new state and would have to leave the region. They were not happy, to say the least, and said that they would fight the separation. They were whistling in the wind, their voices would never be heard except by me and I had no power or influence. I had to obey the rules like everybody else.

I set up my office in the local government building and started setting up a registration for people to get onto the electoral roll. People came by the hundreds and then thousands as the word got out that there would be free elections; it was a freedom from the Raj, a freedom that everybody wanted. They wanted to be like Britain and have a democratically elected national and local legislature. I had a couple of council officials to help me but they were really overworked.

I drew up a constitution document that would cover local government and submitted it to Mountbatten, to be added to the draft I had previously been involved with. I also sent a copy to Gandhi who would rubber stamp it regardless of what Mountbatten would do.

The structure of Governance also interested me. I was unsure about the head of the country. Would it be an elected post as per the American model, or would they stick with the British monarchy who didn't require election? Below this tier would be an upper chamber or Senate. I guessed that would comprise one or two representatives from each of the states and the main body of Government. I would need to look at breaking up the state into thirty or forty regions, each with its own Member of Parliament. Then below that would be the Local Government. Each region would need to be further broken down. I needed a map of the region so that I could do that.

I arranged to have meetings with the local police chief, the Chief Medical Officer at the only hospital that I found, and the local judiciary. We had put most of the structure in place but what we didn't give India was a political structure. Everything else would continue until such time as the new central government changed things. What really worried me was the maharajah, and Nasri was still coming into my thoughts in my quiet times. I wondered how she was, where she was, and I guessed that she was already married. Fate had brought me to her doorstep only to find that she was no longer there. I asked around and the police chief told me that she was married to a prince in the south of the country. It was unlikely that she would return to her family home here in Jurihadnapur. I was left to sort out the political arrangements.

Back in the central office, I found that my predecessors had done most of my job for me. I sought out the previous governor, who was just packing his bags to go back home to England. He was a middle-aged man with grey receding hair and a rotund appearance. He had been there for twenty years. We had afternoon tea together and I found out that he actually knew Nasri, but that news came at the end of our conversation, after I had tried to sort out some form of electoral register. He was convinced that the Indians would never be able to self-govern as they argued too much amongst themselves. This I was already finding out.

He gave me what papers and maps he had of the state and he wished me luck in trying to put in an electoral system. He was looking forward to a well-earned retirement in rural Worcestershire. He would be in for a shock when he arrived back in England, I thought. It was not the rural bliss that he had left twenty years before. The world had moved on.

I took what papers and maps I needed and had them delivered to my office in Government House. I was becoming used to the fact that, in India, there was always somebody there to do my bidding.

This gave me some homework and, having arrived at some sort of breakdown, I decided to cover the country myself, to get the lie of the land, so to speak. This took longer than I expected. The poverty was appalling but despite this everybody seemed to have a smile on their face. I doubted whether they could read or write. I saw the local police chief who explained the local set up. He was surprised when I explained that every man and woman over the age of seventeen would have a free vote and needed to be registered. He would need to protect the small team of lawyers that I appointed to carry out the task.

This simple exercise took nearly two months. Next was trying to bring the political factions into some sort of order. I was undecided about whether to see them individually or collectively. Collectively won the argument, as I didn't want to engender what could be construed as favouritism. The meeting was set up for one evening at eight o'clock, when it would be cool. I also invited the maharajah. I had no idea whether he would turn up or not.

The appointed day came round, and all the party leaders and their close helpers attended. They were all assembled in the main chamber and they were already arguing amongst themselves when I arrived. I tried to bring order without success. In the end I needed to resort to less diplomatic measures. I took my Navy revolver from its holster and fired a shot over the heads of the arguing assembly. It had the desired effect as everybody suddenly stopped talking.

'Gentlemen, ladies,' I said, 'this is not the place for a debating chamber. I have gathered you here this evening to give you information that you will all need to get to grips with. I have no favouritism and am totally impartial.'

I then went on to explain the electoral voting process and also the timescale for Independence. I would have preferred ten years but it would be less than ten months. The British Government were determined to push the process through. I tried to explain the separation, but this was met with a deafening silence. An elderly gentleman on the front row stood up to address me and the assembly.

'Sir, we appreciate what you are trying to do and we have no argument with you, only between ourselves. I think that we are on the brink of a once-in-a-lifetime opportunity, and I hope that passions do not get too heated, but we are a passionate people. I think that I speak for all political parties when I say that we will give you our co-operation in trying to achieve your aims.'

He sat down.

'Thank you for that reassurance,' I told him, 'but this will happen whether I am here or not. I have spoken to Gandhi and this is his wish for you all: he wants a lasting peace between Muslims and Hindus. There have been riots and many, many deaths in Calcutta, and he is currently on a hunger strike and will starve to death unless this conflict ceases. I don't want your small community to add to his departure from this life. I don't like separation but it is the price that both sections of your community have to pay for independence from the British Government, which is what you really want. I will do all in my limited power to facilitate a peaceful and orderly movement of families and communities.'

There was a muttering around the members present.

I concluded my speech. 'There is only one last request from me, and that is for you and your supporters to encourage ordinary people to register to vote. I have been around the state and the police and local authorities have been advised and ready. Many of your supporters cannot read or write but they too have the right to vote. I am giving you the task of making sure that this right, which has been hard won, is not wasted. The meeting is ended. Please go in peace.'

I left the podium. I didn't want any questions or to be involved with any of the politics that they were now formulating. I had an evening walk in the garden at the rear of Government House. I hoped that it would be a peaceful process but my guess was that tempers would flare up. I was at a loss as to why that happened. They seemed to be happy in what little they had. Maybe offering them something they had no concept of was just expecting too much when it could deliver little or nothing. I retired to bed. The maharajah had not showed but I guess that he knew all about it and had received a first-hand report.

I wasn't wrong. The following day I saw his messenger, who requested my company at the palace at four. I sent him away with another message: the maharajah would have to come to me. I would not be visiting the palace any time soon. I wondered whether he would bend to my authority. He didn't turn up. I guess that I had upset him. It was something that he would have to get used to.

About a week later the maharajah came to my office late in the afternoon. Everybody made way for him as he strode into my office. I ignored him until he stood before me, trying to intimidate me.

'Ah, Your Highness,' I said as I looked in my diary. 'I have a full diary for today and you have not made an appointment. Could I ask you to see the secretary at the door and make an appointment?'

'You may not. I am here and here I will stay. *You* get out,' he said to my companion, exerting his perceived power and authority.

I stood up. 'Stay where you are,' I told the person sitting the other side of my desk, then I turned to the prince. 'You, Sir, have no authority here, and for a man who is supposed to have good manners and stature you have shown that you have none of these qualities. I would ask you again to leave and take your turn in line with everybody else. Failing that I will call the police and have you thrown out.'

The maharajah went puce with rage. He had never been spoken to in these terms. I guessed that he would have to get used to just having one vote, like everybody else in India.

He turned, shouting at me. 'You haven't heard the last of this.'

I let him go, sat down and returned to my discussion with the man in front of me. That news would go round the community faster than any telegraph ever could. I had reduced the perceived power of the Raj and if I could stand up to him, so could everybody else. This was the power of independence.

A week later that the maharajah came to my office again. This time he had made an appointment and the secretary had given in to his request to clear my diary of all other appointments. I wondered what he had to say.

He was shown into my office. I stood up to greet him.

'Please take a seat and tell me how I can help you.'

He momentarily stood his ground, before taking a seat and waving his minder to leave. This was to be a private conversation. I waited for him say something.

'Commander Jones, you need to tell me what you are doing,' he said.

'I don't have to tell you anything, but will concede that you would like to know how your sphere of influence is being diminished.'

He was not altogether happy with my response but wanted to know more so waved for me to carry on. I continued.

'Your estate and business activities will not be affected in any way. What Gandhi wants is a clear independence from the British Government. He is putting in place a political system roughly based upon the British system with possible elements of the American constitution. Each man and woman will have just one vote to use as they choose. You have the same right. That's about it. What is troubling everybody is the time scale. This time next year, you will have total independence, whatever that means.'

'What is your role? You are a Naval Officer and not a lawyer or politician.'

'Can I refresh your memory? Eight years ago you visited the Rolls-Royce factory and I had the dubious pleasure of your company when you came to Cambridge to bring your daughter back here to marry her betrothed husband.' I reminded the maharajah of our previous meeting.

'And you were that young lawyer who had found favour with Nasri.' He nodded as he remembered.

'Yes, the daughter who you unloaded onto a man whom you perceived could advance your interests,' I told him. 'It was not a good choice. He is being stripped of his power as I am now advising you to take a more humble role in life and put your ostentatious living to one side. Gandhi will rule this country and he holds no store in worldly goods and wealth.'

'Have you met Gandhi?'

'Yes, we are both lawyers and have a common sense of right and wrong. I missed out being called to the bar when the war started. I enlisted in the Royal Navy. I still serve my King and country with Mountbatten, who also has a Naval Commission. So there you have it. If I can help you in any way, I offer my services to you.'

'I can see that I have totally underestimated you. Now I don't know what to do,' he admitted.

'Do you remember what I previously told you? I will help you but I don't make the decision for you. That is your responsibility. My opinion is that you need to move out of your palace and take a smaller dwelling somewhere in a quiet part of your estate, and take on a simpler lifestyle that will be looked on favourably when Gandhi becomes President, as he surely will.'

'What would I do with the palace? Nobody would buy it.'

'Turn in into a hospital or a school. Give something back to the community and you will gain a love and respect that will replace the fear and resentment that they presently have for you. I also think that I have done you a great disservice by throwing you out of here. From now on, everybody will stand up to you and not fawn in your presence.'

'Yes, that has already happened. I have been humiliated whenever I've appeared in public.'

I stood up. 'If there is nothing else, I have much to do and little or no time to do it.'

'No, I think that all my worst nightmares have come to fruition.'

He stood and I walked with him to the front door where the Rolls-Royce was waiting for him. Somebody had thrown a raw egg at the car and it was still running down the passenger window. Resentment was now raising its ugly head.

I let him go and returned to my office to continue writing the letters that seemed to be a never-ending activity.

The days and weeks passed as I became totally immersed in putting in an electoral process. I had a couple of trips to New Delhi where, together with other regional actuators, we compared notes and tips on how to deal with difficult locals. I had just one further visit to Gandhi, who looked frail and gaunt from his enforced hunger strike. I asked him about the palace being turned into a hospital and school. He nodded his appreciation. I guessed that it would be used as a model and the staffing would be just a formality. It was the last time that I ever met the great man.

Back in Jurihadnapur I returned to making sure that everything was ready for elections, and asked people to step forward for nomination. Despite the fact that communication was so poor, I thought that I did really well. It was a slow process but that was about all.

The maharajah took my advice and moved out of his palace, into a modest villa in the hills that overlooked a wooded valley. He invited me to see him. I accepted the invitation and he sent a car for me. It was *the* Rolls-Royce that I had previously seen in Cambridge. I ran the gamut of abuse. At one point the crowd in front of the car stopped any progress. I stepped out of the car to address the crowd. They stepped back when they saw that it was me in my naval uniform and not the maharajah. I raised my hand to try to get some sort of quiet.

'Gentlemen, I am not worthy of your anger. I am a servant of the British Government and have only one task ahead of me: to give you independence and autonomy. This car is a symbol of British Rule. I will take it back to England with me when I leave in a few weeks' time. I am sorry that you have such bad feeling towards me when all I want to do is implement Gandhi's wishes. The great man is not in good health and I don't want to report this to him as he will be saddened by your lack of respect for me.'

The crowd parted. I returned to the back of the car and we drove on. I was shaken by the anger of the crowd. I had my revolver with me but only six shells to confront what appeared to be at least a hundred angry men.

At the villa, I was met by the maharajah in a white cotton suit. He offered his hand and I accepted, taking a firm grip.

'Come inside. I have a surprise for you.' He invited me into the cool entrance.

Waiting there was Nasri! She smiled when she saw me. She was still the beautiful young woman that I had fallen in love with eight years earlier but now stood before me as a married woman. I held out my hand to shake hers.

'Jeremy, you look well and the uniform suits you,' she said. 'Come into the garden where tea is being served.'

I looked around and the maharajah had left us. I followed Nasri into a sheltered courtyard where there were hanging baskets and flowering plants, giving shade and liberating perfume into the air. Afternoon tea was already prepared and waiting for me to make an appearance. We sat down and a servant poured me a cup of tea.

'You are quiet. Cat got your tongue?' Nasri asked as she sipped her cup of tea.

'I'm surprised to see you,' I admitted.

'Daddy telephoned me and told me that you were here in Jurihadnapur, dragging us into the 20th century. I wanted and needed to see you again.'

'It was not on my agenda to have afternoon tea with a married princess.'

She put her cup down. 'Ah, so that's what's in your craw.'

I stood up. 'If you will excuse me, I have to leave as other business needs my attention.'

'No, it doesn't. I've travelled the best part of two days to come here just to see you. From what Daddy told me, I was surprised and pleased that you accepted his invitation. Aren't you pleased to see me?'

'Do you want me to answer that honestly?' I asked.

'Yes! I always thought that my wealth and position were always working against me.'

'Nasri, our worlds collided. We were never meant to be anything other than passing acquaintances.'

'I fell in love with you and that hasn't changed despite my being married to a man that I don't know and don't like.'

'I'm sorry to hear that,' I said. 'I don't think that ever entered your father's head when he made the arrangement.'

'No, it was taken as read and I just went along with it. Every woman in my family has had an arranged marriage. It was just accepted that I would follow suit.'

'I need to leave. Would you please arrange for the car to take me back?'

'Can I come with you?' she asked.

I was taken aback at the request.

'What would your father say?'

She stood up. 'I am no longer his ward and he has no influence or authority over what I do or where I go. My husband might, but he has turned his back on me. Maybe I should tell you now that I might have had to share his bed but he has never been able to get me pregnant and he has given up on me for a younger woman who will bear him sons that he will be proud of.'

'So why haven't you got a family?'

'Didn't want one. I wanted your children and when I realised that would never happen I didn't want any from anybody else. My years in Cambridge gave me everything I needed regarding contraception. I was a big disappointment to my husband and after only three months he made alternative sexual arrangements.'

'Oh, I see.' I couldn't think of anything else to say.

'Are you married? Is there a woman in your life that I don't know about?'

'No and no. I am a confirmed bachelor and am pursuing a career in the Royal Navy. When this present tour of duty is completed I shall be posted elsewhere, wherever I am needed.'

Nasri smiled at me. 'Shall we go?'

'I will leave you here and I have no intention of returning. Thank you for the tea and the use of the Rolls.'

She threaded her arm through mine. 'Jeremy, I love you and don't understand why you are so cold towards me.'

'Maybe because I still love you and you are even further away from me than when we first met. Now, I am leaving without you.'

I turned and walked through the house to the Roll-Royce that was still waiting for me at the front door. I went and sat in the back seat. The driver came scurrying over and we set off back to my residence. I had no idea why I had been so cold towards Nasri. She had done nothing other than admit her love for me. That was all that I did not want; a distraction in the form of Nasri.

My work load increased as my desire to complete it diminished. Meeting Nasri again had really upset me more than I cared to admit. I realised that the inertia of moving to independence was now inevitable regardless of what I did or didn't do. I tried to put Nasri out of my mind but she was always there.

As the days and weeks passed the big day loomed ever larger. Everything was in place as far as I was concerned. We had the voting forms. We had all the candidates. We had all the ballot boxes and counters arranged. There seemed little or nothing left for me to do. I had an unexpected visit from the maharajah. He seemed resigned to his new position in society. This time I greeted him and invited him to take afternoon tea with me. All the anger and anxiety had evaporated. My days in India were now numbered and he wasn't the only one who was losing power and influence.

He sat with me and after the usual pleasantries he reminded me of our long-ago conversation in Cambridge.

'You and I have some unfinished business,' he reminded me.

'Perhaps you would jog my memory.'

'We need to have that cricket match.'

'Ah, do I sense that you are issuing me with a challenge?'

'Exactly. I was thinking of a Maharajah's Eleven against a British Eleven.'

'Hm. It might turn out to be a Royal Navy Eleven.'

'Even better. I was thinking of booking the New Delhi Oval and making it part of the independence celebrations,' he said.

'What will we play for? There must be some sort of trophy.'

'It could be something as simple as the match ball. If you accept this invitation, I would suggest a 20-over match where each man in each team bowls two overs and you and I start the bowling as well as open the batting.'

'Do you have any other demands?' I asked.

'No matter who wins we can have a grand banquet in the evening. It will be a fitting end to mark your departure, as rivals and friends rather than vanquished oppressors.'

'I will call Mountbatten. Damn it, I'll do it now, if you will excuse me.'

I went to my office desk and put in the call. Mountbatten was delighted and accepted the invitation to be one umpire, the Indian Chief of Police could be the other. I went back to report to the maharajah.

'Jones, I'm sad that we have been at odds with each other. I think that we had the makings of good friends and I've only recently realised that you are an honest man doing an impossible job.'

'I think that you're right about me having an impossible job but I would have difficulty coming to terms with claiming you as a friend,' I told him.

'Let's hope that the cricket match will sort things out. There is one other thing. I want you to buy my Rolls-Royce, the red and black one.'

I was surprised. 'What would I do with a car? I'm in the Navy and likely to be floating around the world until the end of 1948.'

'I would accept an offer of one guinea. Will you buy it?'

'For one guinea I don't think that I could refuse. I will take it up to New Delhi after the elections. It will also give me an opportunity to learn how to drive it.'

He leaned across and offered his hand. The deal had been made and settled. I needed to get my hands on a gold sovereign.

We left on the best of terms. I needed to practise my bowling skills; It was a much needed diversion. I drew a wicket on the garden wall, found a cricket ball and spent an hour a day bowling my off breaks. I also found a bat and took my house boy to bowl at me, hoping that I could hit the ball. I only had one stroke and polished that. I didn't have any pads and it concentrated my mind to hit the ball and not let it rap me on the shins. My legs were black and blue but I still persevered.

The week before the voting day, I had a late afternoon visit from Nasri. She drove to see me in the red and black Rolls-Royce.

'Hello, Jeremy, I've brought your car. If you drive me back I will show you the idiosyncrasies of Rolls-Royce.'

'Before or after tea?'

'After if you don't mind. I don't know whether the news reaches you but I have been helping to set up part of the old palace as a school and we open in a couple of months. I will be teaching English.'

'I was expecting you to go back south to be the faithful and loving wife.'

'I will one day, perhaps, but there seems to be much to be done here.'

'My days are numbered. I will be moving on to my next assignment.'

'Do you have any idea what that will be and where?' she asked.

'None at all, but I'm sure that Mountbatten will keep me close to him for the remainder of my tour of duty.'

'I've heard about nothing but the cricket match that my father is organising.'

'Yes, Mountbatten will be an umpire and he is trawling, for want of a better word, the Royal Navy for as many ringers as he can find.'

'What's a ringer?'

'An expert in one thing who is employed doing something else. There must be a few top class cricketers in the Navy, it's just a matter of finding them. It takes our minds off the job we are doing. Will you be at the match?'

'Yes. You know that there is a banquet after the match to which I am persuading Daddy to take me along. I am hoping that you will be my escort for the evening. He has already approved of that and I am hoping that you don't veto it.'

'Ah, part of the *entente cordiale*. I can't see how I can refuse such an honour.'

I was more relaxed with Nasri than I had been for weeks now, and our friendship was again blossoming. We had a pleasant afternoon tea together, that moved on to dinner. I welcomed her company, someone that I could have a conversation with. I wasn't concerned that there was another agenda I was not aware of.

When it was time for her to leave it was just getting dark, which was not the best time to have a driving lesson, but it was only a relatively short journey and we slowly trundled along as I familiarised myself with the controls of the car. She asked me to stop a short distance from her home. I pulled over to see what she wanted.

'I have something for you,' she explained.

'Do I have to guess or is it a surprise?'

She smiled. 'We need to sit in the back.'

'Why not here?' I asked.

'Jeremy, back seat, please.'

I gave in and we went to sit on the soft cloth seat in the back of the car. She sat close to me and leaned across to put her lips on mine. So that was the surprise she had for me! I found myself responding, putting my arms around her. It was everything that I had ever wanted and my conscience left me, abandoning me to her love and affection. I was totally immersed in her beauty, and intoxicated with her perfume. I was a lost soul. When she whispered 'Make love to me' all my good intentions evaporated and succumbed to my overwhelming desire to make her mine.

It was really dark when our kissing became affection rather than mutual passion. We struggled to find our clothes, getting hurriedly dressed and hoping that we looked presentable, not as though we'd had a close intimate encounter. We moved back to the front of the car to complete the journey we had started an hour or so before. At her residence I walked her to the front door of the villa. She gave me a quick kiss before turning and leaving me on the doorstep with a car that I really didn't need or want, yet which had taken on the symbol of the altar where I made the ultimate sacrifice. I drove slowly and carefully back to the hotel, parked the car and went to bed with Nasri on my mind and her perfume still on my clothes and being. I slept like I had not slept for months, in fact since I had arrived in India.

I didn't see Nasri again before voting day. I had a Cook's Tour of a few polling booths and then spent the night overseeing the counting as the ballot boxes started to arrive in the Government House. I went to bed hoping to get some sleep. I was awoken in the early morning to hear the election results. There were disappointments, and elation for the few that had been elected, and then there were speeches before everybody left to celebrate or just go to bed. I had a last day in my office submitting my report on the validity of the election, and announcing the winners.

I had breakfast and collected all my belongings together, ready to have them loaded onto the carrier on the back of the Rolls. It would be a long slow drive over very poor roads to New Delhi. I arrived late at night and was pleased to find my bed. It had been a very long two days.

Next day I reported to Mountbatten, who was delighted that everything had passed off so well. There had been a few incidents that had been expected but by and large everybody seemed satisfied. It would be a week before all the results were in, and the handover was arranged for the following week. There would be a formal handing over of power from Great Britain to the new Indian administration, then we would have the cricket match followed by a banquet. We would then evacuate our quarters, leaving everything in the hands of the newly appointed Ambassador whom I had yet to meet.

There was a cricket joke going round, where being captain of the cricket team was the only naval captaincy that I would ever have. Mountbatten enjoyed the joke as he told me that he had made an application for me to be made a Rear-Admiral working out of the Ministry of Defence in Whitehall. The only ship I would ever see would be the ship taking me back to England.

I was kitted out in my Commander's uniform and was included in the inauguration parade. It was mighty hot in my full uniform but I was not the only one feeling the heat. Mountbatten carried the occasion off with all the grace that it demanded. It was a big anticlimax for the British contingent and we were all looking forward to the cricket match. Evidently, tickets had been sold and there were several thousand spectators to witness the last act of the British Empire.

I drove to the ground in my Rolls-Royce and parked it near the players' entrance. I made my way to the visitors' changing room and met up with my team. They were of various rankings, from an engine room stoker who was our 'ace in the hole' fast bowler, upwards. All formal ranks had been put aside for the match. I explained the agreement I had with the maharajah. It was widely accepted and we met up with the opposition over lunch, when both teams were introduced to each other.

At the appointed time, dressed in whites, both teams made a tunnel where the two captains strode out into the middle of the pitch. I produced a brand new gold sovereign that I handed to the maharajah, who handed it to Mountbatten. He flicked the coin in the air and I called heads. It was tails. The maharajah chose to bat first. We would be out in the field in the heat of the day; it was not a good toss to lose. I picked up the coin and handed it to the maharajah. 'This is the outstanding payment for the Rolls-Royce.'

He took the coin with a smile. 'Thank you. It will be a lasting memento of this occasion.'

I went to my team to announce that we were bowling first. We retired to the changing room where the wicket keeper put on his pads and, with our caps on, we went into the field. I was bowling the first two overs from the pavilion end to the maharajah, who strode out padded up. He was really up for giving us a good hiding. So the match commenced.

My first over was better than I expected, as only four runs were taken off me. My bowler at the other end went for seven runs, leaving me to bowl to a free-swinging batsman who I thought I recognised as being in the Indian test team. So this was their ringer. My first ball he hooked for six. For the next three balls I tried to spin as much as I could and had some success with the turn as he only got one away for four. Having spun the ball with some turn, the fifth ball I just bowled straight with top spin. He anticipated the ball turning and missed; the top spin kept the ball low and it hit his leg pad dead plumb before the wicket. I appealed for lbw and it was confirmed. I had my very first wicket but I only had one ball left. So I had figures of 14 runs for one wicket. That would stand forever in my annals.

The rest of the match went from good to bad, and back to good. Our fast bowler took two wickets in his two-over spell for only four byes that the wicket keeper was unable to stop. It all ended when the Maharajah's Eleven made 62 runs. We all left the field and drank as much liquid as we could take on board. It had been really hot out there on the field. Later in the afternoon there was a slight breeze and the temperature started dropping. I was padded up and, pulling my cap down over my eyes, I made my way out to the wicket. I faced the first ball from the maharajah and, with my best forward defensive stroke, pushed it back to the bowler. This continued more or less all through the innings. All the runs came from my team members at the other end. We lost wickets at an alarming rate, until it came down to the last wicket in the last over and the last ball. We needed six to win, five to tie. Anything else would hand the win to our opponents. I didn't know what to do. I only had one shot and had only picked up a couple of runs, pushing the ball back and blocking everything. The bowler ran up and delivered a fast ball. I had nothing to lose and swung my bat at it, making perfect contact. Unfortunately, I had hit the ball towards the furthest boundary where, with just one bounce, it went over the rope. It was a four. We lost the match by one run.

Both teams came onto the field, where there were handshakes all round and I took the match ball and handed it to the maharajah. 'Let this be the trophy,' I announced. He produced the ball they had used and handed it to me. There were no losers in this match. We were all winners.

We had afternoon tea, both teams mingling. That evening we all

THE BLACK AND RED ROLLS ROYCE

dressed for a formal banquet with wives and girlfriends. I had Nasri on my arm, which was the perfect end, and it didn't go unnoticed that the good will between Britain and India was cemented for all time.

After the banquet, I escorted Nasri back to her hotel, where we had a nightcap together. I stayed the night with her. I wished that it could have been longer but she was leaving the next day, going back to Jurihadnapur, and I would be on my way back to England on the next boat sailing from Bombay. I would drive there and arrange for the Rolls-Royce to be delivered to my parents in Norfolk.

It was a long drive, on roads that were no more than tracks in some places, and paved roads with an unbelievable amount of traffic of all descriptions. I went through villages, towns and cities. I had to wait a couple of days in Bombay before sailing back to England. It gave me the opportunity to arrange transport of the Rolls-Royce by freight steamer back to Tilbury.

It was five weeks later that I landed in Plymouth, and then onward to London and Whitehall. I was given extended leave which gave me the opportunity to collect the Rolls-Royce from Tilbury and have a leisurely drive along the East Anglia coast to Norfolk. My parents were surprised and delighted to have me home, with my new status symbol.

I had to leave the Rolls with my parents as I reported for duty in the Ministry of Defence, only to be told that I now had a promotion to Rear-Admiral and needed to get my new uniform. I had an office and an adjutant but nothing to do other than visit the bar to enjoy pink gins.

I didn't see Mountbatten and I spent my days reading *The Times* and keeping up with current affairs. I was shocked when I read of Gandhi's assassination. It gave me doubts regarding the fragility of the new democracy. I felt helpless and worried about Nasri. I was still in London and unable to exert any sort of influence. I became sad at my further loss.

Just before leaving the Navy, I had afternoon tea with Mountbatten at the Foreign Office. I wondered what that was all about. Mountbatten wanted me to come under Atlee's attention. It was the week before my commission came to an end and I was summoned to the Foreign Office for a meeting with the Minister, Ernest Bevin. He was an out-and-out Socialist, a trade union man who seemed not to fit the mould of Secretary of State. He explained that we needed a High Commissioner in a Central American Dependency and I had been shortlisted for the post. If I accepted the office, after a short spell of leave I could take up the post.

I was delighted as it meant my service in the Diplomatic Service was secure. I accepted without reservation. I would have to attend briefings on the political background and all the varied local elements, from Catholics to Black Magic and everything in between, as well as the local War Lords and their followers. It sounded like a powder keg that was about to explode. I had been given a poisoned chalice and this was my baptism into the front line of British Colonial life. I would do my duty for King and country.

I left my post in the Ministry of Defence and spent a couple of weeks with my parents. They wanted to know of my future plans. I didn't want to alarm them but told them that I had accepted the post of High Commissioner at a Central American Dependency. They were proud to hear that. All idea of me becoming a barrister had long since passed.

I was concerned that the Rolls-Royce needed attention and took it to the local garage, who only confirmed my suspicion that it needed an overhaul. I had driven it over too many unmade roads and the suspension and steering needed to be replaced. It would take some time as the parts had to be specially ordered from the manufacturer. I departed from Southampton before the car had been repaired. It would be garaged and ready for when I returned.

CHAPTER SIX

My American adventure, for that's what it turned out to be, was one of unexpected danger and confrontation, dealing with the most unsavoury characters this planet has ever produced. Well, in my eyes anyway. It was exactly as I expected, the Catholic Church and the Jesuit priests in particular seemed to hold the population to ransom. Can I say at this point that I have no serious objection to any religion or religious order other than when I see some sort of injustice. I had frequent meetings with the Archbishop of the country, as I did with the political leaders. They all seemed to want power and money, or was it money and power? Whatever the whys and wherefores, the country was in a mess, with corruption leading the way. To add to the problems, in the neighbouring state there had been a very violent and bloody uprising, ending with a coup where one barbaric dictator was replaced by an equal equivalent.

I was invited to join the new leader for exploratory talks. What he really wanted was a secure border, and also recognition of the new regime. All I could offer was to put his case forward to the Foreign Office who would take the matter up in the United Nations. As for the border, I requested at least one battalion of an artillery and infantry soldiers with a token gesture of tanks.

I was summoned back to London to the Ministry of Defence where the Chiefs of Staff explained to me why armed warfare in the jungle was not even a remote possibility. We were already committed to leaving troops in a divided Germany and there was trouble brewing in the Middle East. We would follow America's lead, whatever that was likely to be. I would get a few foot patrols for the main crossing points and that was it. I would have a frigate call in when in the area doing patrols; nothing more.

I returned to my official residence in dismay. The Foreign Office did nothing. It was nothing to do with them and it was left to other South American States to make representations. I felt isolated.

This came to a head when the local activists, spurred on by the apparent success of their neighbours, sought to overthrow the British and get us out. They were very nice about it. They wanted power and money like everybody else and they saw the British as just getting in the way of their ambition.

I woke up one morning with the 'Freedom' fighters camped outside on my lawn. I went out to ask what they were doing. I was told to stay indoors and mind my own business if I wanted to stay alive, and not to even think of going anywhere. After a few days I met with their leader who, to my surprise, was well-educated and spoke perfect English. I told him that it was preposterous that he keep me and my staff in some sort of imprisonment. He said that it would only be a temporary arrangement and that when he had negotiated a peace with Britain I would be free to leave. In the meantime, for my own safety it would be best if I stayed indoors. To my surprise he let my staff leave to collect groceries and other items while under strict protection from his men.

It was all very strange and I had little choice other than stay in my residence or go out and get shot. It seemed that I had no choice at all if I wanted to stay alive. I had no contact with London or the outside world as the rebels had taken over the telephone exchange. I had no idea what was going on. I guessed nothing.

This situation lasted, would you believe, for two years. Little or no progress had been made by the coup and it all ended when a frigate and a couple of troop carriers turned up and within a few hours had liberated not only me but the country. I was again summoned to London to make my report. It fell on deaf ears. They were now committed to fighting a war in Korea. Central America had little significance and our military was stretched beyond breaking point.

I took the trouble to see my parents. Unbeknown to me, my father had been taken ill with pneumonia and died within a few days of being diagnosed. My mother had sold the family home and moved to a small sheltered housing apartment. I had to stay in a local bed and breakfast.

I went in search of my car, only to find that the garage no longer existed and my car had disappeared into the ether. Nobody seemed to know anything other than the garage owner had been killed in a freak accident, the business closed and all the assets and liabilities disposed of, including my car.

What a mess. But I had little time to dwell on it as I was relieved of my position in the Caribbean. I realised that they didn't sack diplomats so much as put them where they could do least harm. I was despatched to a group of Pacific Islands at Tokelau. It took eight weeks to get there and I discovered they came under New Zealand Territories. I was in a South Sea Tropical Paradise. The girls only wore grass skirts for ceremonial occasions, all other time they just wore a cotton wrap, and more often than not went around half naked. The men likewise only wore a wrap-around skirt, but they were physically strong and muscular. They mainly lived off the sea, with fruit from the abundance of trees. Their favourite dish was sucking pig. It really was a strange diet but one I would get used to.

We had a weekly visit from the steamer that came from New Zealand bringing post and supplies. I entertained the captain, to have somebody British to talk to and to glean whatever news there was regarding the rest of the world. The captain was more interested in bedding one of the local native girls than talking to me so, after a couple of trips, our meeting was set for an early dinner with little or no conversation.

The only other English people on the island were a middle-aged Methodist Missionary minister and his sparrow-like wife. They wanted me to attend Sunday Services and I went once a month. Most of the population were Catholic and their religious instruction was through a Jesuit priest who also ran the school. I think that the local population took to Christianity in the vain hope of getting to heaven as well as continue with their own beliefs. On one island in the group, they had a strange mix of disbeliefs that were in line with a God that provided them with things like ball point pens. How did the ink get into the pen? It must be the God that Westerners worshipped. It was a Cult Cargo. Maybe not, but they thought if they worshipped the same God, these things would come to them.

We also had what I considered a 'town' drunk except we didn't have a town. I think that he originated from Liverpool but had jumped ship or had been thrown off one and had landed up on an island paradise. His one attribute was that he had the tendency to make an alcoholic beverage that he distilled into hard liquor. To make this more palatable, he mixed it with local fruit flavourings but it still had a kick like that of a mule. He would call round frequently, mainly just before the steamer was due in. What he wanted was all the bottles that had been discarded. He made a good and profitable living from selling his illicit booze to the Lascars working the boats, as well as to the locals. Once in his cups he would tell garrulous and ribald tales of his time at sea. He had run away from home at fourteen and went on a boat to Brazil. When he came back as a man of the world, his father beat him and sent him back to school. At least he was harmless and entertaining.

I had annual visits to Auckland to report in, and managed to catch up on whatever first-hand news there was. The years came and went and altogether I was there the best part of twenty years. There were highlights, of course. I entertained Her Majesty the Queen on her one and only visit to the neighbouring island of Tonga. She knighted me on the steps of the Royal Palace. That sounds rather grand, really it was no more that a very large thatched hut where the local royalty resided, but it was an honour that I cherished.

My mother died and I didn't find out until weeks later when the post arrived, eight weeks after posting in England. I was saddened that I had not been there for either my father or my mother but I guess that was the price that you had to pay for being in the Diplomatic Service. I really hadn't thought that through. I should have returned to Law and had an interesting and challenging life in the Inner Temple, strolling round to the Old Bailey with visits to Lords and the Oval for cricket test matches. Now all I did was listen to complaints of land and rights and other offences that I passed on to the local police to deal with. They didn't have a jail. The islands were jails of a different sort: there was nowhere to escape to.

One day, quite unannounced, my replacement arrived with his wife and young family. I turned my house over to them and spent the following week going through the various legalities that were to be his responsibilities. I had to wait for the next steamer that would take me back to civilisation.

It was two months later that I disembarked the steamer in Tilbury Docks and caught the train up to London. I took a room at the Army and Navy Club until, as Mr Macawber put it, something turned up. And turn up it did.

I paid my respects to the Minister in the Foreign Office, only to be told that I had been retired from the service some six months previous but had never received the notice as it was still sitting on a clerk's desk. However, due to my long service both in the Royal Navy and the Diplomatic Service a Grace and Favour house, or rather an apartment, had become available in Bloomsbury, if I was interested. Was I interested? Bet your boots I was interested, and within three months I had moved into an empty shell. I had great pleasure in strolling around the Portobello and Notting Hill markets, picking up quality if well-used furniture and fittings to equip my new residence. I found a cleaner. She was a middle-aged lady who liked to look after her gentlemen, of which I was one. She kept me honest, not only dusting and vacuuming but taking my laundry and bringing it back clean and well pressed. As for cooking, I had a strange repertoire of meals that were mainly vegetarian and fish. I really had been out of England too long. And then one morning the auction catalogue dropped on my door mat.

CHAPTER SEVEN

It was a bright fresh morning in Harrogate. I had a hearty breakfast at the Majestic Hotel before making my way to the Pavilions on the Great Yorkshire Show Ground. It was all very nice, with flower beds full of colour and neatly trimmed lawns. The car park seemed to be full already as the would-be buyers were having a second look at what was on offer. I registered my interest and was given a number on a card. I didn't have to shout out my name should my offer be accepted. I wondered how much I could afford. The anticipated £2500 seemed within my reach, but more than £5000 and the car would not be coming home with me. As the clock moved towards two o'clock, people started taking their seats in front of the lectern, waiting for the appearance of the auctioneer. I was standing at the back, waiting with nervous anxiety.

My mind went blank as I took in the scene opening up before me, when I felt a hand take mine. I spun round to see who was invading my space and had a double-take. Before me was an Indian lady with a silk scarf over her head that draped over her shoulder. She was wearing a long colourful dress. Her dark eyes seemed to be dull but her smile was warm and welcoming.

'Jeremy, it is you,' she said.

I was stunned. 'Nasri, what are you doing here?'

'Waiting and hoping that you would turn up.'

'So, it was you who sent the auction catalogue.'

She tugged my hand. 'Can we go outside? It's rather crowded in here and when the auction starts we won't be able to talk.'

'I don't want to miss the Rolls-Royce coming up.'

'Jeremy, you won't miss anything, believe me,' she said as she kept hold of my hand and led me out into the sunshine. We walked slowly along the path between the lawns and flower beds.

She stopped, and turned to face me. 'Now you can kiss me as if you have missed me. You have missed me, haven't you?'

'Nasri…'

Before I was able to make any response to her question, I found her in my arms and her lips on mine. Long moments later we continued our walk arm in arm along the path.

'I really need to get back to the auction,' I persisted.

'No you don't,' she said, and she opened her other hand to show me a gold sovereign. 'You have already bought the car once so there is no point in trying to buy it again. It's already yours. I've withdrawn it from the auction.'

I stared at her. 'I don't understand.'

We found a park bench and sat down, holding hands. I needed Nasri to tell me what I wanted to know, but she spoke first.

'Jeremy, I need to bring you up-to-date with all sorts of things, and I need you to tell me everything that has happened to you since I saw you last.'

'We don't have that much time but I need to know why you are here.'

'Firstly, Joffi died ages ago. I think the young concubines that he brought into his palace wore him out. He disowned me as a wife and I returned to Jurihadnapur. As you probably recall I started setting up and teaching English at the new school. That lasted until Father died and I was left with the estate to run. I had tea gardens and each year I come over to visit Newcastle, Manchester and Harrogate to see the tea buyers. That's what brought me here.'

I took in this information and thought it through. She was now a widow and not a separated married woman. It eased my mind, regarding the morality of my association with a married woman, but I didn't have time to dwell on this as she was continuing her narrative almost without a pause.

'And now I've found you here,' she was saying.

'Tell me about the car,' I asked her.

'It was the key to finding you, although I didn't realise that when I found it and that was purely by accident. I read in the paper that a Rolls-Royce had been discovered after being in a farm shed for over twenty years. There was a photograph of the car and I recognised the number plate. I found the farm and made the farmer an offer on behalf of the owner, namely you. He was pleased to see the back of it and I then gave it to a car restorer. After two years we had a ride in it. I drove it and it brought back a whole load of memories, particularly with you and the back seat.'

'I can't believe that you have reminded me of that.'

'Why not? We both loved each other and what's wrong with that? Nothing.' She looked at me, with her dark eyes searching out my true feelings. She was right, of course.

'I have been trying to find you for years,' she said. 'Nobody seemed to know what had happened to you. I went to Norfolk, only to find that your father had died and nobody knew what had happened to you or your mother. I started searching out Jeremy Jones. Have you any idea how many I found? Six. I didn't have the courage to trawl around Wales asking after you, so I came up with an idea. I would put the car into an auction and send the catalogue to all the Jeremy Jones's that I could find. Only one Jeremy Jones would recognise the car. It was just a long shot that you would turn up, but you have and at last I've found you.'

'You should start a sleuth agency,' I told her. 'I think that you would be really successful. I can't believe that you have been looking for me for twenty years.'

'Are you married? Have you never met another woman to share your life?'

'No. I fell in love with you, and circumstances took me first into the War Office and then to India where I met up with you again. After that I went to Central America and was caught up in the middle of a civil war, and that's when I lost the car. After failing miserably in the Diplomatic Service I was sent somewhere I could do no harm and was in the South Pacific for the best part of twenty years. I have never met anybody who I wanted to share my life with. But the car restoration must have cost you a small fortune.'

'It was worth every penny just to have you back in my life,' she said, smiling.

'I had no idea what had happened to you. I was sent to a dot on the map and I arrived back here with no job and just a small pension. There was no way that I could afford to travel anywhere outside the United Kingdom.'

'I guessed that you were still as poor as a church mouse. I have developed my father's estate and am living a comfortable life, albeit alone. I fell in love with a clever and handsome undergraduate. He was the only man that I ever loved and I wanted no one else. I realised that I could wait forever and wait in vain for you to come for me. I had to find you and so that's what I've done.'

I sighed. 'I fell in love with you and it seemed that fate got in the way at every turn. I was resigned to having a loveless life without you. And you are right, I was never in a position to come to find you. I thought that you were married and that would be for life.'

'Can we start where we left off in India all those years ago?' she asked me. 'Or do we have to go back to the very start when we met in Cambridge?'

'I need to start again from where we are now.'

'Where are you staying?' she asked.

'The Majestic. I've packed my bag and left it with the concierge. I didn't know whether I would be leaving tonight or driving back to London tomorrow.'

Nasri smiled a knowing smile. 'I'm also staying at the Majestic, and was preparing to drive to Cambridge tomorrow. I would never have let the car be sold to anybody else.'

I shook my head in confusion. 'Now I don't know what to do.'

Nasri continued to smile. I guessed that she was going to make my mind up for me.

'Jeremy, check out of your room and move in with me tonight. It is something that I have wanted all my adult life, and at last we have the opportunity. I can't believe that you don't want the same.'

I laughed. 'You are a wicked woman suggesting such a thing, but I will gladly accept your invitation. Now, can I buy you afternoon tea?'

'Yes,' she said, 'but dinner would be preferable. I would like you to come with me to Cambridge tomorrow. We can share the driving. I was wondering what to do with the car; I think that I have now found a solution.'

'And what's that?' I asked.

'It's yours and you can do whatever you want with it, but I would rather that you kept it rather than sell it on.'

'It was never my intention to sell it and I was quite distraught when I lost it. The garage where it was being kept closed down and I never found out what had happened to it.'

She kissed me lightly. 'It's settled then. We can collect the car tomorrow and you can come with me to Cambridge.'

We got up from the bench and telephoned for a taxi to return us to the Majestic. I checked out, collected my bag from the concierge, and moved into Nasri's suite. We didn't make the dining room but had room service and a bottle of champagne. I realised that my love for Nasri had not diminished, and she still had a firm place in my heart and affections. She was determined that we would not be separated and wanted to see my apartment in London. I was unsure whether she would be returning to India or staying with me in London, but I guessed that we would never be separated again.

We collected the car from the Pavilions and the auctioneer was not pleased at losing his commission. He approached us with the ignition keys.

'After the sale,' he said, 'I had an American potential buyer who was interested in the Phantom I Rolls-Royce. He is here now and would like to have a word with you.'

'Are you his commissioned agent?' I asked.

'I'm not at liberty to answer that question.'

He didn't have to. His response was all that I needed. I think that both Nasri and I wondered what the interest this other man had in the car. We were introduced to a tall, slim American who approached us and shook our hands.

'I believe that you are the owners of the Rolls-Royce that was removed from the auction yesterday,' he said.

Nasri replied for me. 'Yes, Sir Jeremy Jones is the true owner and this is Sir Jeremy.'

He turned to me. 'I'm pleased to meet you, Sir, and would like to make you an offer for the car.'

'What's your interest in this particular car?' I asked.

'It is the least modified version in original condition and I represent an Auto Museum in Massachusetts. I have flown over just to buy this vehicle and have authority to offer up to a value of $50,000.'

Wow, I thought, they must really want this car. That figure would surely have covered all the restoration costs. I looked at Nasri and realised that, although she had given me the car back to do with as I wished, she didn't want me to accept what was, for me, a small fortune. I knew what she wanted.

'That would be a generous offer but I'm afraid that car is not for sale, now or in the future. What I will do, with the princess's permission, is give the vehicle to the museum without charge when both of us have passed on.'

My announcement brought a smile to the lips of Nasri and a surprised look to the American's face.

'That could be years down the line,' he observed.

'I sincerely hope that is,' I told him. 'I have no desire to leave this mortal coil in the near future.'

He turned and left, realising that his mission had failed in the short term but the museum's money would be safe in the bank for another project.

We collected the car and drove it to the Majestic, where we loaded our bags and commenced the drive to Cambridge.

The car performed beautifully. It really liked the tarmac roads rather than the bumpy cart tracks that had wrecked the suspension and steering on my drive across India some twenty years previous. We broke the journey at the George Inn in Stamford, where I quizzed Nasri about why she was going to Cambridge. I was in for a shock.

'Jeremy, I have a confession to make to you,' she told me. 'I have a son. He is studying Law at Churchill in Cambridge. I am going to meet him and I want you to meet him.'

'Why didn't you tell me before?'

'Firstly, I didn't have the opportunity as I didn't know that I was pregnant when I last spent time with you, which you will remember was at the banquet after the cricket match.'

I was silent as this information sunk in. It raised all sorts of questions, like who was the father? I thought that it was most likely the late Joffi and wondered why she hadn't known when she was with me, or did she go back to him? I had no idea.

'Jeremy, Jamil – that's his name – is your son. After our unrestrained and unprotected love-making in the back of the Rolls, I conceived. I have wanted to tell you and for you to meet him… and…'

'Mine! My God!'

'I'm sorry to have dropped that on you but I wanted you to know,' she said.

'Does Jamil know?' I asked her.

'No. I will tell him tomorrow, when he will meet you.'

As the journey continued to Cambridge, I was able to ask Nasri more about the boy. It was a simple story: he was interested in doing something useful for his country, to put something back into India as a developing international nation. He chose to study the law himself. Nasri had never told him about me. She had told him about his grandfather's cricket match and about buying and selling the Rolls-Royce, but had never told anybody who the boy's father was.

We checked into the University Arms for the night, and after dinner we had our second night together. I realised that this was something that I had always wanted but hadn't realised how much more it was than I could ever have imagined. I thought about whether I wanted it to continue? Yes, I did. I wanted more, not less, or even worse, nothing. Having been given a vision of the promised land I was now in it and didn't want it to end, or for me to let it go. I knew that I would need to make some sort of commitment and hoped that Nasri would say 'Yes'. And I had a son!

It was bright, late Spring morning when we drove the Rolls from Parkers Piece up to the front steps of Churchill College. Nasri announced herself to the porter, who scuttled off in search of Jamil. We stood by the car waiting for our son to make an appearance.

When he came down the steps I had my first sight of my boy. He was tall and slim with a shock of jet black hair and his mother's dark eyes. He had a coffee-coloured complexion and looked fit and healthy and surprisingly well-dressed for an undergraduate, compared with my days as a student with my well-worn slacks, holey woollen sweater and long, unkempt hair.

He broke into a broad smile as he greeted his mother with a kiss on the cheek.

'Jamil, I would like to introduce you to Sir Jeremy Jones,' she said. 'He's an old friend of your grandfather and was his adversary on the cricket pitch.'

He moved towards me and shook my hand. He was about to say something when Nasri interrupted his thoughts. 'Jamil, Jeremy is your natural father.'

He stopped what he was about to say and looked from me to his mother and then back to me.

Nasri continued. 'Jeremy has been abroad for the past twenty years and we only met up again yesterday.'

'He's my father?' was all that Jamil could say. He was in shock.

I stepped forward and put my arms around him and kissed his cheek. 'Yes, I truly am your father. I have loved your mother for over thirty years. The war came between us and I have only just met her again, and only learnt about you yesterday so I'm in shock as well.'

Jamil didn't know what to say but tears were rolling down his cheeks. 'Mother never told me.'

'No, I don't suppose she did. There is something that I need to do that I should have done many years ago.'

I turned to Nasri and took both her hands in mine. 'Nasri, I love you, I always have and I always will. Will you marry me?'

Tears of joy filled her eyes.

'Jeremy, JJ, I've never stopped loving you and yes, I will marry you. I want us to be a family and not three individuals. We all have much to catch up and we might as well start now.'

C.S. SIDAWAY